TWO FATES

Judy is a single mother who has no real achievements to her credit. She quit her advertising job to write full-time and be a stay-at-home parent. *Two Fates* is her first book through which she hopes to become famous, sell movie rights and fight with Aamir Khan. She's currently a freelance writer who is also involved with theatre and is an avid blogger.

Judy and her daughter live in Chennai. For more about Judy and her writing – www.judybalan.com

TWO FATES

The Story of My Divorce

Judy Balan

westland ltd

Venkat Towers, 165, P.H. Road, Maduravoyal, Chennai 600 095
No. 38/10 (New No.5), Raghava Nagar, New Timber Yard Layout, Bangalore 560 026
Survey No. A - 9, II Floor, Moula Ali Industrial Area, Moula Ali, Hyderabad 500 040
23/181, Anand Nagar, Nehru Road, Santacruz East, Mumbai 400 055
4322/3, Ansari Road, Daryaganj, New Delhi 110 002

First published in India by westland ltd 2011

Disclaimer
This is a work of fiction and not the story of *my* divorce.

10 9 8 7 6 5 4 3 2 1

ISBN: 9789381626009

Typeset by Arun Bisht

Printed at Manipal Technologies Limited, Manipal

For my parents
for never trying to be cool.
They are.

Contents

Acknowledgements

I'm deeply thankful to . . .

God for never giving up on me, for keeping His promises and 'making all things new' through Christ, His Son.

Kiara, my five year old, for being my biggest fan and telling all at school, 'My mamma wrote a book, you know?'

My mum for being my all-in-all support system and pushing me in the direction of my dreams (as opposed to what's 'practical') long before it became fashionable.

My brother Rajiv who forced himself to read *Two States* though it's not his genre – just so he gets all my jokes. Also, for being the man I most look up to.

My dad who wanted me to become a software engineer (ha, ha) but graciously settled for writer.

My grandparents for being consistently and obnoxiously proud of all my achievements since kindergarten. And for all the love, prayers and support.

My paternal uncle who conjured up the best stories for us (my brother and I) when we were children. I hope he enjoys this.

Andaleeb – without whose constant nudging, pep-talks and blind faith in my abilities, I would have never even thought of writing a novel, let alone finishing it and taking it seriously enough to send it to publishers.

Acknowledgements

Meera – who read the book first – on a busy day at work – and gushed every ten minutes about how much she loved it. Also, for mildly (very mildly, I promise) inspiring Twinky (don't kill me).

Avinash – I stole his smile and even a couple of his endearing (or not) traits for Rishab. Also, for being one of my early readers and giving me honest feedback.

Uncle OT, Revathi, Taran, Roxana – some wonderful people I met on my blog – who read the manuscript literally overnight, gave me constructive feedback and cheered me on to the end. Taran, for patiently enduring my elementary questions on Punjabis and teaching me how 'bhindi' is spelt.

Swapna and Fr. Ignatius Prasad – for their support, prayers and for being my angels in every sense through my own divorce.

Venu and Deepa – for always being there – be it for exchanging ideas or just a chat. Venu for being my very own Dumbledore.

Blog readers, friends, family and well-wishers who've eagerly awaited the book – I hope it doesn't disappoint.

My cousins Deepika and Nithya who were the only ones in the family to read the manuscript. Deepika, for being cutely thrilled about sharing her name with my protagonist.

The nosy strangers, the petty aunties (I don't speak of people I'm actually related to here *cough* *cough*), the bimbettes, the self-proclaimed cool dudes, the readymade-advice-dispensing know-it-alls – I never thought I'd say this, but boy, am I glad for my share of run-ins with them! *Two Fates* wouldn't be half as entertaining without the characters they inspired.

My editor and the people at Westland and Tranquebar Press for their faith in my work.

And of course, Chetan Bhagat – without whose novel *Two States – The Story of My Marriage*, this book wouldn't be.

Prologue

'I have nothing to say to you,' he blurted out as he sauntered into my office.

I tried not to roll my eyes given that he was my fifth patient from IIT that week. He made himself comfortable on one of the bean bags that lay at odd angles on my wooden floor, even before I could gesture to him to sit down. I studied him while he took a sweeping glance at the fuschia pink wall that faced my desk. Clad in a clean pair of blue jeans and a neatly pressed white shirt, my disoriented, but otherwise perfectly normal-looking patient, appeared too old to be in college. His eyes darted across the room as if he was searching for something.

'No accolades adorning your walls for my reassurance?' he asked me.

'No, I'm modest like that,' I said. He was beginning to annoy me already.

'Siddharth,' I said repeating the name on the brief given me by Totu, his cousin. 'Call me Sid,' he said and adjusted his glasses quite unnecessarily.

Controlling the urge to roll my eyes again I continued, 'So you're from IIT-IIM.'

'Yes, though I passed out years ago,' he replied, finally putting an end to my inexplicable urge to slap him.

You see, my last four patients from IIT had all just passed out of college and had what I un-fondly call, The Gandhi Complex – a delusional condition that often makes the patient imagine that the future of the nation rests squarely on his shoulders. Common symptoms include smugness, narcissism and heightened patriotic fervour. In extreme cases (such as my previous four patients), it leads to demoralization on account of not being able to meet the self-imposed pressures of changing the future of the nation. In fact, my previous patients were all battling with suicidal tendencies and by now, I was in half a mind to assist this one on his suicidal mission. But thankfully, his story was different.

'So why has your cousin mentioned that you're from IIT if you passed out years ago?' I enquired, a touch annoyed.

'I don't know. They always do,' he answered in a matter-of-fact way.

Now the urge was back. To slap him, of course. The smugness was getting to me.

'You're a psychotherapist,' I cautioned myself. 'You can't afford to be temperamental.'

'No, you're just a psycho,' the voice in my head interrupted.

Siddharth stared at me and I don't know if he caught me looking spaced out while I was having my self-talk, but he seemed amused. I quickly put on my thick, black-framed glasses that I used to intimidate patients. Against my pearly complexion and jet black mane, they really did stand out and not in an empathetic-doctor kind of way. I drew the curtains and when the room was sufficiently dark, I settled on my recliner.

'So, what's your story?' I put on a deep, chocolatey voice to unnerve him.

But Siddharth or Sid as the pretentious bastard liked to be called, was unfazed.

'My three-year marriage has fallen apart and my wife and I would like to go our separate ways.' He sounded bored.

'Our families though, are unwilling to let that happen without a fight, and fixing a meeting with you is their idea of getting me to change my mind,' he continued coolly.

I looked away from him and stared at my fuschia wall – taking deep breaths and praying for the patience to endure him. His eyes shifted curiously from me to the wall and back to me, as he enquired if I was all right.

'I can't let a patient ask me if I'm all right,' I thought. 'What do I do?'

'Spook him,' the voice in my head said.

'So talk to me, Sid,' I said choosing a more airy, high-pitched voice this time. But I might as well have worn layers of beads and sat in front of a crystal ball, because that's how seriously he seemed to be taking me.

'Tell me how you two got here,' I persuaded.

'Well we don't get along. That's really all there is to it. Our minds are made up. We want a divorce,' he rattled off at jet speed.

'That shouldn't be hard,' I thought. Aloud.

He raised his eyebrows quizzically to indicate I wasn't supposed to say that, but seemed pleased about it nonetheless.

'So you're not going to advise me on saving my marriage?' he asked, suddenly taking an interest in the session.

'That depends,' I answered. 'Why are you here if your mind's made up?'

'To please my family, extended family, some well-meaning friends, the neighbours, the milk-man, his cow and some aunties who saw me last when I was eight,' he answered with a hint of pride at his own talent for sarcasm.

'What would you like me to do for you?' I enquired, cutting to the chase.

'Assure my family that you tried, but that you believe I have good reason for leaving the marriage. Can you do that?' he responded, his eyes fixed on me like a beady-eyed terrier.

'I could, but it will come at a price.' I spoke slowly for added effect.

'I'm aware, five hundred rupees,' the smart alec retorted.

'Not that,' I answered with an evil grin.

He looked puzzled.

'I will tell you *my* story and *you* will listen,' I told him.

'What? *You* want to talk to *me* on *my* time?' he snapped in disbelief.

'*You* want a favourable report from *me*?' I shot back, totally enjoying my moment.

'You are mental,' he said and sat back in his bean bag, sulking like a kid who had to do his homework before playtime.

I was thrilled at the thought of telling my story even if it was to a captive audience. The fact that he was from IIT only added to my joy. You will see why later.

'Don't sulk so much, there's a lot in it for you,' I assured him.

'I bet,' he breathed. 'What, are you about to tell me how to get the elders to consent to our divorce?'

'Maybe,' I answered, still smiling at my novel idea of therapy.

He sighed. 'So what's your story?' he asked resignedly.

'The story of my divorce,' I whispered. In a come-hither fashion by mistake. Luckily, he didn't notice.

'You're divorced?' he almost squealed in a mixture of delight and bewilderment.

I was excited myself, to have finally cracked this case.

'Shhhh. Now listen or I'll exceed my time and *you* will pay more,' I warned him.

He didn't seem to care. The beady-eyed terrier look was back on. I had his undivided attention.

Act | 1:

Delhi & Chennai

One

We were at his cousin Sweety's wedding reception, bickering continually as we stood in the buffet queue. The line seemed as endless as the number of food stalls sprawled across the freshly-mown lawn of the four-star hotel. The Punjabis really went the whole hog and splurged unjustifiably on weddings. It often upset my prudent-with-finances Tamilian sensibilities, but tonight I was distracted by the gradually mounting wall of hostility between us. He stood before me in the line and I looked closely at his steadily-receding hairline, his gold-rimmed glasses and general IIT smugness, wondering exactly what I had seen in him just a couple of years ago.

'We're out of rasgullas,' the man behind the counter announced.

I sulked. It was my favourite on the menu. In fact, I could have a whole meal with just rasgullas.

'But we have *gajar halva*,' he said gleefully, dumping a large lump of the tacky, orange sweet on my plate before I could protest. I wrinkled my nose and nibbled on a spoonful as I watched Rish thoroughly enjoying the last rasgulla just an arm's length away. And that's when it hit me – it was over. He had said a lot of mean things to me the past few months including a persistent suggestion to see a shrink, but nothing made things quite as clear as this. You know your husband doesn't love you anymore when he stops sharing his rasgulla with you. Miffed, I dumped my plate and walked in the opposite direction when I ran into his cousins – Bunty, Mitu, Kitty and Lotu – all wanted to know why we were both acting weird around each other. I cringed slightly at the thought of how obvious we had been. I used to be fond of his cousins before, but suddenly everything about them grated on me like sandpaper.

'People with names like that shouldn't be allowed to speak, form opinions or come out in public,' I thought to myself before politely requesting them to ask their *bhai* themselves. Rish sat alone lost in his own world probably dreaming of becoming a writer and stealing my thunder, when the cousins swarmed around him making their signature cackling noise, that I knew embarrassed him. For a whole half hour they needled him with their questions without any success.

'Rishab,' I said finally, joining him after they left.

'Deepika,' he acknowledged right back. Using the full first name was safe. It meant the relationship was strained as opposed to 'Rishab Khanna' and 'Deepika Sundar' which spelt mortal danger.

'We need to talk,' I continued.

'What about?' he asked in his signature passive-aggressive style. I wanted to slap him then and there. I hated it when he pretended like nothing was wrong.

'About us making passionate love all the time and waking up the neighbours,' I said drilling my hawk eyes into his seemingly docile, brown ones.

'There's a nice room just upstairs,' he answered and as his wife of two years and partner of five, I knew he wasn't spewing sarcasm. He was just thick. And yet, *he* was the IITian and I was the literature graduate he had been 'short-changed with'.

I wanted to pull my hair out in frustration, but managed a 'let's just get out of here' before storming out through the plush corridors of the hotel.

We remained silent in the car for the first five minutes. This was not normal for us though, because we usually preferred hurling insults at each other to wallowing in our misery alone. So I took the initiative.

'I hate the noise in your family weddings and I think I'll barf if I see another set of index fingers pointing up at the sky to the tune of Daler Mehndi,' I started. 'I won't be coming to the next one.'

'Perfect. One tight-assed Tamilian less to deal with,' he retorted.

'I know. You guys are such a fun bunch,' I said and he waited for the sarcasm to hit a crescendo. Not wanting to disappoint him, I added, 'So, what are Sweety and Monty planning to name their kids? Sugary and Syrupy?'

'No, I think they're planning to go with classy, modern names like Ramakrishnan and Rajalakshmi,' he responded with a slight smile.

Honestly, I didn't know why we were quibbling about our communities, when the real problem was just us. We couldn't stand each other. That was the truth. I no longer thought he looked like George Clooney's younger brother and he had developed an obvious distaste for all light-skinned, taller-than-necessary women, right from Julia Roberts to Shilpa Shetty, thanks to me. I also hated the fact that he was trying his hand at fiction-writing which was one of *my* dreams, instead of burying his nose in some IIT-deserving software company in NYC where I could become a famous columnist like my television counterpart, Carrie Bradshaw.

He wanted to paint the living-room walls white. I wanted one wall in yellow. He thought yellow was tacky and typical of South Indians. I thought white was nauseating and typical of hospitals. He brushed his teeth in the shower which I thought was disgusting. I brushed my hair in the living room which he said was grossly unhygienic. I wanted him to hum less. He wanted me to talk less. He could make love any time of the day or night. I preferred it at 8 p.m. on weeknights so it gave us enough time for pillow talk (which *he* insisted on), washing up and grabbing a snack before hitting the sack by 11 p.m. Also, I liked to tidy the bed before we got on it while he didn't mind doing it inside a garbage truck. He thought I was prudish. I thought he was abnormal. He argued that I had changed after marriage. I complained that he had *not*.

I entered the house and fumbled for the light-switch while he parked the car in the garage. I was wracking my brains for one more thing about him that I knew drove me up the wall, but I couldn't remember. Then he entered the house with a familiar expression on his face, and bang. It came to me now.

He thought farting aloud was funny.

Two

I woke up around day-break and tried to make sense of my surroundings as I lay in bed. 'Rish's parents' house, Delhi' I recollected. Still lying on my stomach, I turned my head to the right and watched him as he slept with his mouth slightly open. He wore the same dirty-blue boxers that I once found irresistible, with his entire body wrapped snugly around a pillow that had now replaced me. I looked at him long and hard, unable to make my peace with the fact that it was the same guy I had thought I'd never run out of conversation with. And that was partly true, given that we still conversed a lot. Only our conversations had grown louder and the content, more lethal. He wore his Saarang 2002 T-shirt that I had almost torn off of him just a few years ago, yet now I squirmed uncomfortably at the thought of it coming off and having to come face to face with his newly developing paunch. To be fair, it was too small to be called a paunch. Maybe paunch*let* was more like it. He began to stir and I quickly closed my eyes, feigning deep sleep.

I wondered if he was staring at me now, pondering the same things I had, just seconds ago.

I wore his favourite mint-green boxers too, with my grey tank top. But I wondered how he saw me now. Did he wrestle with questions about how come he had picked me, as well? Or curse himself for thinking I looked like a runway model? Did he notice that my once concave tummy had grown a little more convex? Or that I drooled in my sleep and parts of my anatomy had succumbed to gravity? Just then his hand fell on my rear, moving slowly and hesitantly. I had my answer – the Y chromosome didn't give a damn about gravity or Shilpa Shetty. All it cared about was what was accessible and right now, it happened to be my cute mint-green, boxer-clad rear. I lay very still, waiting to see where this would go. He took my non-resistance for a yes. I went with the flow. Fifteen minutes later, we went to two separate bathrooms for a shower, feeling geared up to face the challenges that another day of hostility would invariably bring.

We sat next to each other at the dining table for breakfast. His mother sat with us and this meant a whole new type of challenge. We hadn't seen his mother after the reception the previous night, as she had come in late with one of her relatives. I expected her to begin an epic discussion on Sweety and Monty's wedding – what was wrong with it, what was right with it, the colour of the flowers, the crispiness of the chicken, the number of extra teeth the bridegroom had, you get the drift. But she seemed rather focussed on us and I couldn't quite tell why it disturbed me so much.

'Here, take another roti beta,' she offered me a pink Tupperware box full of cholesterol-high buttery rotis.

'So Rishu, any good news yet?' she asked her son.

Breakfast, you see, was the perfect opportunity for an Indian mother to intrude in her children's affairs.

'Yes, we're leaving tonight,' he responded annoyed.

'Arre, come on beta. It's been two whole years and it's not like you had an arranged marriage. When is the baby coming?' she continued, this time looking to me for support. I focussed on my rotis and egg bhujia and let him field the questions alone.

'Can I buy you puppies? Will that make you happy?' he raised his voice a little. She walked away, visibly offended with a loud 'humph' to boot.

Parents can be so naive, I thought. Here we were, trying to play hide-and-seek with questions we knew would lead us to a courtroom saying a completely different kind of 'I do', while his mother's biggest heartache seemed to be the fact that we hadn't dragged children into this mess. Also, privacy and space weren't concepts any Indian parent understood, so I checked myself from fighting her every time she threw one of her tantrums. I dumped my greasy plate in the sink and walked back to the room. Rish followed me like a doting husband, knowing that for the moment, his mother was the more tiresome woman to deal with.

We stood in the room, looking at the crumpled bedspread, the pillows strewn all over the mattress, some on the floor. The mint-green and dirty-blue boxers lay overlapping each other. My tank top and underwire bra hung carelessly on different sides of the large cot's head-support and his Saarang T-shirt finally had a tear in it. After a careful assessment of the crime scene, we finally decided to exchange glances. He still didn't look like George Clooney's brother and I could tell with the look in his eyes that he still loathed Shilpa Shetty because of me. We cleared our throats and turned our attention to packing our bags and destroying the evidence. Among the many principles I clung to in life, the sanctity of marriage was something I strongly believed in. And this was the reason cheating wasn't even a thought in my head or for that matter even Rish's, even when we hated each others' guts. This was also the reason we stood in silence that very moment, shuffling our feet in embarrassment.

That was the first of several times that we had meaningless sex, legitimately.

We spent the rest of the day evading each other, till it was time to get to the airport. After that, we just had to deal with the fact that we were going to be cooped up next to each other in an airplane for three hours and thirty minutes. I came prepared with a seven-hundred-rupee best-seller that I had recently splurged on, and I tried to read once we boarded while he pretended to sleep. I knew he was pretending because he always snored in his sleep and he didn't now. After about an hour of this obnoxious high-school behaviour, we turned around to each other at almost the same time to speak. I let him go first.

'We have to talk,' he said, 'about what happened.'

If it was unhealthy for a married couple to not have sex, it was plain weird for a married couple at the brink of a break-up, to make passionate love. I nodded in agreement, trying to digest the fact that I was about to have the 'where is this going' talk with my husband of two years and partner of five.

'We clearly can't go on like this,' he blurted out as if he'd been meaning to say it for years.

'Are we breaking up?' I asked, getting to the point.

'We need to think about it,' he answered awkwardly.

'What's there to think about?' I shot back. 'Did our love-making this morning mean anything to you?'

'Well what about you? Did it mean anything to you?' he got on the defensive thinking I was accusing him.

'No, no silly,' I corrected him. 'I meant, it didn't mean a thing to *both* of us, so is it fair to the marriage that we stay together?'

He looked thoughtful. Sometimes we both cared more for the institution of marriage than we did for each other. And the thought of being the ones to reduce it to cheap sex, was nothing short of sacrilegious.

'Fine,' he said at last. 'No more sex till we arrive at a decision.'

'Right,' I agreed.

It was past midnight when we got out of the airport in Chennai. The roads were damp from the evening's showers and auto drivers demanded almost half our flight fare to take us to Egmore.

'I hate this city,' Rish muttered as we got into the auto.

I was too tired to argue, so I let him whine in peace. I reclined myself comfortably, with my legs propped up against my swanky red suitcase. The cool night breeze, fresh with the scent of rain-drenched earth was just what I needed to drift into sleep. We reached Montieth Court where we lived in twenty-five minutes – record time for an auto journey from the airport, all the way till Egmore. But that's what I loved about travelling late in Chennai – the empty roads, the silence and the crisp, midnight air.

I woke up with a start as the auto screeched to a halt just outside our apartment complex. I walked in as Rish haggled with the auto driver over the price. Turned out, he wanted twenty-five rupees more, because he hadn't expected to drive this far inside Egmore. I shook the gates, trying to wake up our watchman, Muthu. Easily about seventy-five years old, Muthu was a skinny man who promptly fell asleep by ten, every night. This night, Muthu was wrapped snugly in two warm blankets, making the task of waking him up without disturbing our neighbours doubly challenging. He finally came to the gate after Rish gave out a loud whistle and fumbled in his pockets for the keys for the next five minutes. He then scolded us, shaking his head disapprovingly for coming in so late as if we were teenagers who had crossed our curfew.

Rish took the opportunity to mutter and curse the city again with colourful profanities, while I walked on towards the elevator.

'Electricity *illai*!' Muthu informed us that there was a power failure and we both groaned.

We were both tired and cranky about dealing with another work week starting the next day, apart from solving our own marital issues and the last thing we felt ready to do was climb four flights of stairs with our suitcases and endure a whole night without the air-conditioner.

We groped our way through the living room and Rish hunted for the torch. He returned after about five minutes, with a couple of the scented candles I had bought for their aesthetic appeal.

'Those are not meant to be lit!' I screamed.

'Well find the torch then!' he bit back.

We bickered for another five minutes about whose fault it was that nothing was ever in place in the house and then I decided to change and hit the sack. I rummaged through my wardrobe for a while and finally got into my pink boxers and grey tank. I washed my face and got ready to dive into bed. The thought of the next day at work made me want to grab hold of every precious minute of sleep I could get.

'Feel like a drink?' Rish asked, interrupting the to-do list that was gradually unfolding in my head. I looked at the gorgeous bottle in his hand with the 'Absolut Raspberry' label on it and I succumbed.

'Why not,' I said and he fixed me one of his best.

'I need music,' I sighed. And Rish opened his laptop and set it to our favourite playlist.

We sipped our drinks in the candlelight while Floyd sang about two lost souls who swam in a fish bowl year after year.

'For a couple on the brink of a break-up, this is eerily romantic,' I thought.

We hadn't even really argued since the night before. It felt strangely odd. Almost like nothing had gone wrong.

'Maybe we should go on a vacation,' I said out of the blue.

'I thought we decided no sex,' he answered scowling like it was sinful to go on vacation and not have sex.

'Forget I suggested,' I said, suddenly remembering one of the million reasons I couldn't stand him anymore.

'Or we could go to two different places,' he pitched in.

'That's not a bad idea,' I thought.

'I might as well get some writing done,' he continued, reminding me of another reason I resented him.

'Isn't it amazing how IT geeks who haven't even read an Enid Blyton book their entire wasteful childhood, can actually become writers these days?' I snapped, gulping the last portion of my drink, not able to hold the anger in any longer.

'Yes, it's almost as amazing as literature graduates from Stella Maris College hooking up with IITians,' he retorted walking away to fix our second round.

I followed him to the kitchen to grab a snack when he unnecessarily picked on me again.

'Oh, I'm not mixing anything in your drink, don't worry,' he said.

I remained silent.

'It would take more than a little rat poison to extinguish that vacuum you've got for a head.' We shot each other murderous looks, paying no attention to the quantity of vodka that filled our glasses.

'Funny you should say that since the only head you ever use, is the one between your legs,' I finished with a rush that comes from having the last word, even if it *is* lame.

We gulped down at least a quarter of our freshly-filled glasses in one shot as we settled into our respective bean bags. About fifteen minutes later, all the vodka-gulping we did finally hit us. The playlist was now on Santana and I don't know if it was the Spanish or the vodka, but suddenly I was on his bean bag, comfortably plonked on his lap, facing him with my legs on either side.

'I hate your guts, Rishab Khanna,' I whispered, breaking into inebriated giggles as I leaned forward.

'The feeling is totally reciprocated, Deepika Sundar,' he mocked, as we switched from the metaphorical *cats and dogs* to *bunnies in heat*.

Three

Work was more than difficult the next day for reasons other than exhaustion and sleep-deprivation. My high-neck purple kurta did a sloppy job of camouflaging the furious magenta hickey near my collar bone. I walked into Bennet & Cole, the advertising agency that ensured I had no life apart from work. I ignored the giggling interns while I grabbed my morning cuppa from the coffee machine and joined my team of copywriters and art directors.

'Hey there's going to be a briefing in ten minutes,' Matthew, the client-servicing guy announced, bubbling with enthusiasm as usual.

'It's a big account and lots of interesting ideas have come up,' he continued.

'You'll love working on . . .' his voice trailed off as he spotted my hickey, 'this one,' he finished, eyes still on my collar bone.

'Don't act like a moron who's never seen a love-bite,' I barked at him, switching on my computer, when all the girls swarmed around me without warning. One by one, they gushed about my magenta collar bone in a way that only women could. It didn't matter that our brand manager Mayura, was strutting around in a pair of Jimmy Choos that very moment. Today, mine was the to-die-for accessory.

'Deeps I'm so jealous,' Prathiba, our senior visualizer started.

'Yeah it's so cute that you guys are so passionate and in luuuuurve after two years of marriage,' Swetha, our client-servicing executive said dreamily.

Not wanting to disillusion them, I smiled and nodded in agreement, hoping the briefing would begin soon.

'In here, guys,' Matthew called out and I grabbed my book and pencil and dashed into the conference room. I had never been happier to attend a briefing session or get started on a new project. The truth was, I loved writing, though I wasn't sure if becoming a full-time novelist was my cup of chai. But somehow, every minute I spent in advertising, only convinced me more and more that I was in the wrong profession. Still, we needed the money. *I* needed the money. Since my wonderful IITian had suddenly changed his career plans, there was no telling when he would hang up his boots and take to writing. Besides, I didn't want to depend on him given that our relationship seemed to be headed nowhere. I felt the resentment building up inside me as I imagined him writing best-sellers, signing autographs and selling movie rights. This was *my* dream. And somehow he had managed to steal it from under my nose, given that even my daydreams were of *him* becoming a writer.

'He writes like he talks,' I thought in a disparaging manner exclusive to literature students. 'What would he even write about,' I wondered, not able to get off the train of thought. The annoying sound of giggles brought my attention back to the briefing. Everyone in the room stared at me, amused. I had no clue how long I had spaced out.

Then my gaze fell on the product samples on the table. I stared in horror. Turned out our new client was Hindustan Latex and the product that needed to be promoted was a new flavour of condoms. If that wasn't enough, Matthew thought it would be funny to say something nonsensical like, 'Deepika will be heading this project of course, for obvious reasons,' which led to everyone from the VP to the interns, turning my hickey into some sort of point-and-stare modern art piece. I cursed myself a thousand times for not wearing a *dupatta* and promised myself to return the favour to Rish for making me the laughing stock of the entire agency.

By evening, my day had gone horribly wrong and I blamed him. Add a splitting headache and the pressure of a deadline to the equation, and I just wanted to punch him in the gut when he came to pick me up. I would have given anything to have a warm shower and curl up in bed, but it was my parents' wedding anniversary and we just had to go. I got into our fire-engine red Santro and quickly turned off the music.

'Headache,' I warned him, just in case he was planning on picking on me. But of course, Rish never heeded warnings.

'Another dose of your relatives, just what I need on a Monday,' he started.

Without retorting, I closed my eyes and lay back on the seat plotting revenge. What would make his Tuesday worse than my Monday? An equally embarrassing hickey or a kick in the nuts?

'Hickey, the intention is to cause embarrassment, not pain,' the voice in my head said. I agreed. 'So how long have aunty and uncle been married?' he asked, interrupting my thoughts.

'Thirty years,' I answered not sure if it was an innocent question.

'Wow. Thirty years of celibacy, your dad deserves a medal,' he remarked, clarifying my doubt.

'I suppose you got that idea from *your* dad,' I shot back, giving in to the needling.

'Oh never! My dad cheats,' he answered winking at me and I wanted to slap him.

We reached Seethamma Colony, 4th street, where my parents stayed. I always loved the locality – quiet and classy, my parents were lucky to have bought a flat in their heyday, given that Alwarpet was now Chennai's most highly-priced area. We climbed the stairs to the first floor of King's Cross Apartments and found the door ajar. I hated it when they did that. We could hear the noise way down at the car park, indicating a house full of relatives. I bit my lips as I thought of more embarrassment to follow.

'*Va* ma, Deepu, *Va*,' Janani aunty, a family friend, called out.

We entered the house, removing our shoes by the stand. I avoided making eye contact with Rish, because we had a way of reading each other's minds and I wasn't in the mood to deal with his thoughts on my relatives at the time. I waded through bunches of chit-chatty cousins and aunties, trying to get to my parents, when my eyes fell on Reshu periamma – the quintessential dirty-aunt of our family. You know how, in every family there is a fat, uncouth aunt who makes it a point to embarrass the guest of honour at every function, as if it were her birth right? Reshu periamma was that aunt. What's more, she was known to ask newly-weds the traditional 'How did it go' question about their first night, pinch young boys till they turned beet red and discuss bra sizes with very embarrassed uncles around. All our relatives avoided her like the plague, but my parents were kind to her as she had lost her husband (my father's elder brother) young and had the impossible task of raising two sons, single-handedly. I particularly dreaded this night however, as Reshu periamma had missed our wedding and rumour had it, that she couldn't wait to set her eyes on Rish.

'Oh Rish,' I thought to myself, 'you ain't seen nothin' yet.'

My eyes widened in horror as she came bounding in to the living room at the sight of us and before I could come up with an exit-strategy, she went for the kill. Rish's face turned a deep shade of pink as Reshu periamma pinched and tugged at his cheeks like they were made of play dough.

'What a clever girl you are Deepu, you've brought such a fair boy into our family,' she announced, as if it was the biggest accomplishment our family had ever seen.

Thankfully my dad came to the rescue and we ran to wish him and mom. The cake-cutting took place and the relatives urged mom and dad to feed each other the cake, after which the traditional awkward squirming from dad and fake coyness from mom followed. We all then sang Happy Anniversary to the tune of Happy Birthday, loudly and very out of tune, till the neighbour's dog barked at us.

When it was time to attack the food, I made sure I hid myself among the cousins in the balcony, while Rish remained safely tucked under the adoring gaze of Reshu periamma. I took surreptitious glances at them every now and then and felt most pleased that my dirty-aunt had taken the responsibility of embarrassing Rish entirely upon herself. A good two hours went by without anyone noticing my hickey, now a dull shade of purple and I went over to kiss mom and dad goodbye. The party was still in full flow and it was best that we left now, before mom could protest. Mom and dad followed me to the corner where Rish sat timidly next to my overweight aunt. He got up from his chair, relieved to see me for a change, but I could tell he was not going to let this go without revenge.

'Bye uncle, bye aunty,' Rish said and my parents hugged him.

Not wanting to feel left out of all the family affection, Reshu periamma pinched Rish's cheeks again and planted a sloppy kiss so close to his lips that it embarrassed everyone in the room.

'Okay let's go,' I butt in, beginning to feel sorry for him.

But the bastard pointed to my collar bone and enquired with feigned concern for the entire family to hear, 'What's that on your neck?' before disappearing out of the door.

It was field day for Reshu periamma. Thirty-five minutes and several embarrassing questions later, I finally made my way to the car.

'Definitely kick in the nuts,' the voice in my head hollered.

One and a half years later

'I cannot believe you'd do that,' Rish panicked looking in the mirror, one not-so-fine Wednesday morning.

He had an important presentation to make that day, for which his boss' boss' boss who sat in the US headquarters, was going to be present. As a good-luck charm, I decided to endow him with a bright, burgundy hickey in a strategic spot that no collar could hide.

'Oh come on,' I said with a drawl, still lazing on the bed in my black and red, satin and lace lingerie that I had bought specially for this purpose.

'I'm sure your boss would understand,' I continued, examining my little work of art sitting prettily on his neck, satisfied by the outcome.

It had been a long while since our first loveless love-making incident at his parent's place in Delhi and by now we had got accustomed.

'Women are evil,' he spat out. 'What the hell do you want anyway?' he finally asked the question I had been hoping he would face for two years, almost.

'When are we getting a divorce?' I asked him with Zen-like calm.

'Why do we need a divorce?' he asked me with a stupid expression on his face that meant he already knew the answer.

'Because we hate each others' guts and have meaningless sex,' I answered mustering every ounce of patience I had left.

'It's funny,' he smirked, 'how women like you make such a hue and cry about sex in the beginning – making long speeches about how appalling it is that guys can sleep with women without thinking about commitment and when the poor chap finally commits, you *still* find a reason to not have sex!'

'Hey, we've been going at it like bunnies,' I answered, a touch offended.

'Yes, but it has to have *meaning*,' he shot back.

'Rish,' I began, only to hear the door slam shut.

I felt a twinge of guilt at the thought of the hickey. It really was a petty thing to do. But then it wouldn't have happened had he not put me in a tight spot with his relatives a week ago by cleverly diverting their 'When is the baby coming' questions to me, as if *I* was the reason we weren't thinking of kids. I was furious and my plot was well thought out. But unfortunately, I didn't exactly revel in the cleverness of my plan. Rish rushed out of the house in a crisp white shirt, his hickey still bright enough to divert traffic. I wanted to run after him but I was still in my hot suit. Besides what could I do now to make things better for his presentation?

'He'll be fine,' I told myself. 'I really need this divorce.'

'You will get it,' it was the voice in my head again, 'if you do the right thing first, he will automatically follow suit.'

'What right thing?' I said out loud.

'Apologize and make it up to him for your unjustifiable behaviour,' the voice said.

'But of course, I will do that once he gets home. I just need him to face the fact that it's high time we parted!'

'Apologize now,' the voice was being downright ridiculous. I thought about Rish entering a large conference room at Le Royal Meridien. I pictured him standing before the senior-most people in his company including James Smith, his boss' boss' boss. I knew Rish would slice me in two and feed me to our watchman's dog, Ramu if I interrupted his presentation and embarrassed him before his colleagues, higher-ups and of course, James Smith.

'What the heck,' I reasoned, 'I'm having a conversation with myself!'

'Eureka!' the voice said. 'You've finally figured it out! Congratualtions! You are loola!'

'Oh just shut up,' I said out loud again.

'Apologizing right now could make all the difference between getting the divorce now and four years later, but whatever. You don't have to listen to me. I'm just a *voice*,' it said in a sing-song tone.

It was not the most sensible thing I ever did and I'm sure I came across as a neurotic nutcase to the entire management of

Accenture that day, but the voice kept its word in exchange for my idiocy. I got into a pair of jeans, washed my face, dabbed on some make-up and rushed as fast as my auto driver could take me, to the conference room at Le Royal Meridien which was allotted for Accenture. I was stopped by some of the hotel staff, but managed to wade through, in classic Bollywood style. I entered the huge, tastefully-lit room from one of the side doors and every pair of eyes fell on me except Rish's. He was in the middle of his presentation, eagerly pointing at slides to an audience that seemed to be avidly lapping up everything he said. Until I stepped in, that is.

'Uhh, you would be?' a stern-looking school-principal-like man asked me, gesturing to Rish to hold on for a moment. Rish's eyes widened a thousand times as he stood frozen in horror.

'I just need a moment with my husband,' I said feebly, pointing to Rish, 'it's a bit of an earth-shattering situation.'

'What? I'm sure it can wait!' Rish was in utter disbelief.

'No. It will only be a couple of minutes,' I promised and James Smith resignedly gestured to him to go.

'I cannot believe you,' Rish breathed out when we were out of earshot.

'Do you really hate me that much?' he spoke fast, almost in gasps.

'Rishab Khanna,' I started, 'I, Deepika Sundar, want you to know that you are one hell of a stud boy in bed.' He looked flushed, annoyed and quizzical all the same.

'I promise you many more steamy nights, with or without meaning, if you promise to think about where we're headed,' I said.

'If you need some time, we could take a break and come back,' James Smith suggested graciously from where he was seated at the table.

'Oh no sir, we're good,' Rish answered looking back and forth at the entire senior management of Accenture and me.

'Oh and I'm sorry about the hickey!' I added, raising my voice a notch or two, just so that it could carry across to the conference table. 'Sometimes, you can be painfully irresistible.'

'We will go for a divorce by mutual consent just as soon as this conference is behind me,' he hissed, turning a deep pink. 'Now get out!'

'Really?' I asked, happy tears streaming down my face.

'Yes, really! Now disappear before I lose my job and change my mind!' he shooed me away.

Four

'So, how are we going to go about this?' Rish enquired nervously over dinner.

We both sat, knees propped up on the black marble ledge of our fancy modular kitchen – our favourite place in the whole world to read, cook, eat, sip coffee, fight and make up.

'We call a lawyer, of course,' I answered, in a matter-of-fact tone.

'Stop being so thick,' he snapped, dropping his fork on the plate with a clashing sound to emphasize his point. I finally looked up from my bowl of hot Hakka noodles. I really couldn't get his paranoia.

'It's not as simple as getting the family together and making an announcement,' he continued.

'For all you know, they'd probably call the neighbours over too, thinking we're about to give them baby news!'

He was kind of right, but not totally. We were grown-ups after all.

'Relax, Rish,' I tried to sound consoling.'My folks were never too crazy about you to begin with!'

'I could say the same thing about you and my people,' he bit back.

This was clearly not going in the right direction. And 'my people' was the watch phrase. I knew Rish used it only when he got defensive. Besides, why were we bickering about our communities again?

'Okay, that really wasn't supposed to come out like that,' I attempted to steer the conversation back in the intended direction.

He was silent, but at least he picked his fork up again, which was always a good sign that he was returning to normalcy.

'I meant if we could convince them about the marriage, we should be able to do the same about the divorce,' I continued.

He thought for a while and nodded.

'Fine. I hope you realize this might mean an indefinite stay in Delhi, convincing my mom,' he said, dumping his bowl in the sink.

I didn't like the sound of it, but I didn't want us going back and forth on the divorce itself, and we had waited long enough, so I nodded in reluctant agreement.

The g-strings didn't come out that night. Or ever again, for that matter. Rish decided to watch a movie in the living room and crash on the couch. I lay awake in bed trying to come up with a plan. How would we approach my folks? What would mom and dad's reaction be, precisely?

The more I thought about it, the more I was convinced about Rish being right for once. This was going to be no easy task and we had to make sure we were a team, if we wanted things to go smoothly. And more importantly, we needed a plan. Like the one we had for our marriage. I remembered the many nights we spent strategizing over STD calls on how to break the news to our parents.

Rish and I met under the weirdest of circumstances. I was playing agony aunt to a classmate who had just broken up with her boyfriend and no, Rish was not the hero's friend who stood by him while he belted out mournful Hindi numbers, but the arrogant bastard who had convinced him to dump my poor friend, on the grounds that he 'could do so much better'. It was a classic Pride and Prejudice situation – Mr Darcy talking his best friend Mr Bingley, out of marrying Jane Bennet.

Only, I didn't do justice to Elizabeth Bennet, by staying loyal to my friend and asking Rish to go suck an egg. I fell in love with him instead. And from Pride and Prejudice we moved into a more intense Romeo and Juliet type of phase, only we weren't prepared to die. We thought Tamilians and Punjabis just had some basic cultural differences and were no Capulets and Montagues. Until of course, our families met and put a post-modern spin on the star-crossed lovers – which is to say, they didn't bring out their swords and javelins, but assaulted each other anyway, with some very inventive insults. Rish's mother insisted on wondering aloud about which fairness creams I could have used to turn out as light-skinned as I did. My mother of course reciprocated by asking her how much money her husband had to shell out to get her son into IIT.

In short, there was work to do and several eye-rolls later, Rish and I realized we needed to be qualified to be able to tackle our families. Was there a course on bullshitting our way through impossible situations? But, of course. A whole year and a half of intense preparation later, we both managed to crack the CAT and end up in IIM, Ahmedabad. How did it go? Great. We had all the privacy in the world and far away from our nosy parents. What's more, we were learning the language of the suit-and-tie guys and in a matter of two years, every big name in the corporate world would be standing in line to pay us sinful amounts of money. That was our first year.

I still remember our first day – we had to pretend like we didn't know each other and it drove Rish up the wall as he watched every guy on campus asking me out. He complained that I was too nice in telling them off and that I shouldn't smile so much. So I made a deal with him. He had to give me his share of rasgulla every day and I wouldn't indulge my admirers. Ah, those were good times. By the time we hit the second year, we had too many arrears, so we decided to keep our focus on the task at hand – convincing our parents. Besides, we had learnt enough of the secret language of bullshitting anyway, so the course was no longer of any use to us. We decided to drop out. And how.

Rish feigned a bad case of manic depression, replete with fake suicidal attempts and I played the faithful girlfriend who never left his side. Rish for his part, did an impressive job of returning to normalcy every time I was around and feigning depression and popping anti-depressants (mint), the minute I left. Before we knew it, the job was done. Getting married couldn't have been easier. He didn't have to suck up to my dad and I didn't have to convince his mother about my bhindi-making skills. Because unlike the Capulets and Montagues, it turned out that our parents really did want our happiness and we had just demonstrated to them, that we were inseparable.

So, though the idea of marrying from another state was initially frowned upon by both sides of the family, we did a thoroughly convincing job of acting inseparable and making the Two States idea appear fantastic. Thanks to IIM, we even managed to get them to think it was *their* idea, in the first place. The wedding was a huge hit, especially among younger cousins from both sides, for the bi-cultural theme while our parents were thrilled to be at the receiving end of all the compliments – 'Such an educated boy' and 'Such a fair girl' from my relatives and his, respectively.

A truly unusual thing happened soon after though. Our in-laws fell hopelessly in love with us. I mean, we were grateful enough that they accepted the idea, but they went the whole hog and flaunted us to the world. And what's more, flaunted each other. My parents took Rish's mother on several sight-seeing tours throughout Tamil Nadu, introduced her to relatives as the most affable *samandhi* a parent could ever ask for and Rish's mother for her part, spoilt mom with her culinary specialities, expensive sarees and even bragged about her 'exquisite dosas' to disinterested relatives.

That's the thing about Indian parents-in-law. They only hate you till you're married (unless of course, your mother-in-law whiles away the afternoons watching soaps and is primed to believe you're the villain). After that, they don't just accept you, they smother you. And if you're not smart enough, own you. You are privy to every family secret much against your wishes and even expected to take sides with your mother-in-law against *her* nosy in-laws.

Now, you may or may not get used to these sudden and often, heavy bouts of affection, but rest assured, the rest of your family will. And before you know it, your cousins will be writing to his cousins, your little brother will be in love with his niece and your family will be planning their next summer vacation in Goa along with your in-laws – with or without you. It's almost like the families get married and you become a redundant part of the equation. So the catch of course is that, divorce is out of the question. They don't care about your happiness anymore. They care about theirs. They've found the sibling slash friend slash soulmate they never had in *your* in-laws and they will *not* let go without a fight.

I checked my phone for the time. 3:04 a.m. I turned to my side and willed myself to sleep. I had a long, mentally exhausting day ahead.

Five

Rish looked thoroughly rattled as he shook me awake at about seven in the morning, with a cup of coffee and two words – 'Mom here.' It took me a good five minutes to open my eyes and process what he had just said. I gaped at him blankly and he wasn't helping much by just standing there without saying more. I gestured to him to sit down and he meekly obeyed, looking more flustered than when I had barged into his presentation before Accenture's senior management.

I finished my cup of coffee as he sat taking deep breaths and went to the bathroom to complete my morning rituals. And that's when it hit me, as I splashed cold water on my face – his mom was here. Right *here*. Right now. Why she was here was beyond my capacity to figure out, since we had only seen her a few weeks back *and* she hated travel. Confused, I turned to Rish and he finally managed to open his mouth but tell me nothing.

He had no clue either. All he knew was that he had given his mother a spare key to our apartment the last time she was here and she had conveniently forgotten to return it. What's more, she actually used it to get in this morning and poor Rish was put through an intense interrogation session for sleeping on the couch.

'What did you tell her?' I asked him, a touch anxiously.

'That I was watching TV and fell asleep on the couch,' he replied in a matter-of-fact way and it was the truth.

Yet it sounded lame even to us.

'Did she buy it?' I asked.

'Didn't look it,' he said, looking like a school boy who hadn't done his homework.

I peeped into the living room and found her resting on the couch, so I tip-toed out of the room, while Rish decided to take an hour-long beauty bath. She seemed perfectly still, so I proceeded to the kitchen to fix myself another cup of coffee, when she came up behind me without a warning and plunged into a lecture.

'I knew it. You two are not even sleeping in the same room. How will the baby arrive then?'

I turned around and managed a 'Good morning aunty', but she paid no attention to my obvious discomfort with her broaching the baby topic and my visible shock of seeing her at such close proximity, all of a sudden. Before I could work out a response, she thrust two air-tickets in my hand and continued her rant-a-thon.

'Here. This is why I went ahead and planned your second honeymoon. It's not even four years, but you two seem to need it,' she said, almost spitting the last words out.

'But aunty,' I hesitated, my eyes popping out at the destination. I might have expected Goa, Shimla or even Maldives, but aunty had gone ahead and booked us two tickets to London, knowing full well that our UK visas weren't going to expire for another four months. Rish's cousin Twinky had been asking us ever since we got married to come and visit her in London and then go on a romantic trip to Scotland. A couple of months ago, she decided to send us the necessary documents along with a sponsor letter, leaving us no choice but to apply for a visa. We promptly got the visa, but told her we couldn't take off from work, which was part-truth. I tried to snap out of the shock, when aunty continued.

'I'm not leaving till you both pack your bags and jet off,' she said with finality. And with that, she folded her arms and glowered at me like I was ten. The woman was only half my size, but at that moment, I was nervous. This couldn't be. There was no way I could take off from work and no way Rish and I could stand being together in a place like Scotland that simply reeked of mush.

'Does Rish know?' I asked.

'No, that's your job,' she answered, 'convincing him, I mean.'

'Huh?' I said, my jaw dropping open dramatically, but she ignored me.

I had nothing to do with this and somehow it was *my* job. My mother-in-law was sometimes so good at talking without making sense that she made our one and half years in IIM appear completely pointless.

'But you can't do this,' I blurted out after mustering some courage.

'But I just did,' she answered with a wink and settled on the couch again.

'Remember, not leaving till you leave,' she said as I turned to leave the kitchen, and somehow looked like she meant every word of it.

In the room, Rish stood with his towel still draped around him and blinked a thousand times at the tickets I handed him.

'How the hell are we going to get out of this,' is all he could say after what seemed like ten whole minutes.

'I'm not going. There's no way I can take off from work,' I said.

'Fine, then mom will be here with us,' he said as if this whole thing was my idea.

I could have broken his nose that very minute, but I reminded myself that we needed to be a team.

'Maybe we should just tell her,' I suggested.

'Tell her what,' he spat, almost daring me to say it.

'That we're getting a divorce,' I said.

'Fine. *You* tell her and *you* handle her. I'm off to work,' he said, every bit like the brave, strong man I thought I had married.

I let out a loud, exasperated sigh.

'So, what do you want to do, then?' I chewed every word suppressing my urge to throw something at him.

'We fly to London and then holiday in Scotland,' he answered as if it was the most obvious thing to do.

'You can't be serious.' I couldn't believe him. 'What about your work?'

'I'll work it out. It's the only way to please her and get her to listen to us,' he explained.

I stared vacantly at him. This whole situation was simply ludicrous! I always thought we managed to get away with our *Two States* marriage too easily. It was just bad karma, I told myself. There was nothing we could do.

All the suicidal stories we conjured up to convince our parents, were only reaping for us a long and difficult divorce, including two mentally draining weeks in the most romantic country in the world. I looked at the tickets again. It was booked for the 7th of August 2010 – just a week later. I knew what I had to do. Talk to Matthew, my client-servicing idiot. Tell him the truth about our marriage and the divorce. I even knew he'd understand and so would Ravi, my creative director, but the real issue was just the thought of the second honeymoon itself. It wouldn't have seemed so awkward even a year earlier, with all the meaningless sex and non-confrontational relationship we were having. Why now, after we had managed to get past the silence and decide on the divorce? And why to the one country I always wanted to visit? I felt like the butt of another cosmic joke.

'Bollocks, you're getting a divorce,' Matthew laughed, as I earnestly presented my case.

My quizzical expression was met with many more versions of mocking disbelief – 'If you want to go away with Rishab and get all cute and coochie cooey in some fairy-tale-like cottage in Scotland, just say it na?' Even Matthew, the most cynical guy at work when it came to love, was being completely blinded by our seemingly perfect relationship.

I couldn't believe it. The joke never seemed to end. I stretched myself resignedly on the long, red couch in the conference room where we wasted most of our time, 'ideating'. I stared blankly at a very amused Matthew perched on the pine-wood conference table. He flipped through a magazine and told me all about his bad date the previous night with a girl he had met once at a party. I had barely slept the night before and my thoughts flitted absent-mindedly from Matthew's one-night stands to true love, commitment and divorce. I finally remembered why I was there at the conference room chatting with Matthew and decided I was too tired to convince him.

'Okay, so do I get to go or not?' I asked him at last.

'Good. I like straightforward requests,' he smiled like he knew me best.

'So yes, I will put the new writer on the refined oil job,' he finished.

Grateful, I muttered a 'thank you' before drifting into a blissful comatose, far removed from confrontations and second honeymoons.

Six

It was past eleven in the night, when I reached home and found our otherwise quiet apartment a touch noisy. I decided it was my mother-in-law watching TV, as I made it up the stairs to the fourth floor. Our useless elevator ensured I got my dose of cardio every single day. Exhausted, I wanted to just get in and collapse on the couch, when my mother showed up at the door. If that wasn't surprising enough, she was unusually buoyant like a sugar-high two year old.

'Deepu, come come!' she almost shrieked.

'Shhhh amma,' I said, extremely conscious of our nosy neighbours.

'What are you doing here at this time?' I asked her very softly as I entered the house and closed the door behind me – only to be greeted by my father, mother-in-law, Reshu periamma and her younger son, Arvind. A lost-looking, lanky boy of sixteen, Arvind perennially had his head stuck inside a chemistry book, though on one occasion, I accidentally discovered a James Hadley Chase novel inside said textbook.

I quickly scanned the room trying to make sense of it all – Reshu periamma was laughing hysterically over a very unfunny music video on Sun TV along with my mother-in-law while Arvind was hiding in a corner, reading what was in all probability, James Hadley Chase again. Turned out Reshu periamma had forbidden him from going near Chase on the grounds that he was too young, while she continued molesting the likes of Rish in full view. I rolled my eyes at the irony of it all. I steered my eyes off the right side of the living room and found dad on the divan, quietly engrossed in *The Hindu*, while mom continued acting like a toddler with a lollipop.

'We were just wondering why you kids come home so late,' mom said, as if *that* was the most jarring observation of the evening.

'Anyway, we've been spending all day making vacation plans,' she continued gushing without waiting for my response. Just then, Rish stepped out of the room, wearing his back-from-gym tracks and sleeveless T-shirt. We exchanged a brief, empathetic glance.

'You naughty children, please get naughty in Scotland and give us a naughtier baby to show for it,' Reshu periamma added her touch of crassness to the conversation, accompanied by her usual raucous laughter and obnoxious winking.

Rish looked like he could use her as his treadmill if she opened her mouth one more time.

'Oh God, Reshu you are so funny. You just took the words out of my mouth,' my mother-in-law added and Rish's face turned the shade of my freshly-painted and pedicured toe nails.

I turned around and found dad and Arvind in the same position I saw them when I entered – engrossed in their reading material, oblivious to the inappropriate content of the conversation around them.

'Living with women like mom and Reshu periamma has taught these men coping skills that the rest of us may only hope to learn from self-help books and motivational workshops,' I thought to myself.

'Okay, so here's the plan,' my mom-in-law began, finally directing the conversation at Rish and me. I shuddered at the mention of 'plan'. Hadn't they made enough plans to screw up my whole day and next couple of weeks?

'My sisters Rimple and Dimple thought it would be a great idea to get together here when you kids are off on your second honeymoon,' she informed us eagerly.

Rish's eyes popped out like he had swallowed a fish bone.

'Come where?' he asked in his classic I-don't-know-what-you're-talking-about style.

'Well, here beta! To Chennai! To *your* house!' she clarified.

'They've never seen your place also na?' she added as if that settled the argument.

I just stared blankly. I felt myself growing numb. I would have to be plain daft if I didn't see more unpleasant surprises coming my way.

'So, do you have a plan chalked out?' Rish asked trying to sound like he wasn't in the least agitated about his relatives camping at our place.

'Well I'm not done yet. Kitty, Suhana, Chandu uncle and Raju uncle are also coming!' she announced with childlike glee.

Suddenly Rish had the same resigned, martyr glow that I had. And Scotland seemed like an inviting idea. Actually, the thought of sleeping in the same room with Rish that night, seemed warm and comforting.

'Have you all had dinner?' I asked, in an effort to play the gracious hostess. The three excited women only giggled in response and pointed to the kitchen. On entering, I found the largest stack of Domino's pizza boxes, Kingfisher bottles and one bottle of Smirnoff Green Apple.

Rish joined me at that precise moment and our jaws fell open and stayed that way, for as long as two whole minutes. Suddenly, everything seemed to make sense – mom acting like a sugar-high toddler, my mom-in-law bonding with Reshu periamma and dad quietly hiding behind the newspaper (dad's strong Tamilian sensibilities never allowed him to *enjoy* the drinks he had).

'I wonder how long this party's been going on,' I said finally.

'I wonder how long it will *continue* to go on,' Rish added.

'I can't wait to get to Scotland,' I said.

'Ditto,' he answered.

We finally said goodnight to the family and closed the door to some high-schoolish giggling courtesy Reshu periamma.

'What are we going to do about them?' I asked, hitting the pillow.

It was more of a rhetorical question, but Rish chose to answer it.

'Just sleep and hope they disappear?' he actually smiled.

'Yeah, I'd rather not think of what we'll wake up to,' I said.

'Where will your folks sleep?' Rish asked.

'Do we care?' I said.

'Nah!' he answered and winked at me.

Was he actually cute or was I just deluded? Maybe it was just all the stress, but he suddenly looked as adorable as he used to, back in our Pride and Prejudice days. I threw an arm around him to test the waters.

'You're just stressed, darling. You still hate me,' he said, gently pushing my arm away.

'Go to sleep,' he turned away.

'Bastard,' I said.

He chuckled.

I opened my eyes at 3:20 in the morning and decided to tip-toe to the living room and examine the scene. The couch in the living room was empty. I walked to the guest room and found no one there either. The party was over. Phew. I went back to bed and slept like a baby.

When the alarm went off at 7:30 a.m., Rish was spooning me and his hands were inside my T-shirt.

'You're just stressed darling,' I reminded him, crawling out from under his arms. 'You still hate me.'

'Bitch,' he called out as I made my way to the loo.

I smiled. Sometimes, I let him have the last word.

Seven

'**Y**ou're going to Scotland?' Prathiba shrieked over coffee, when I went over to get my share of the diluted excuse for coffee from our office coffee-machine.

'I cannot believe you girls drink that,' Mayura joined in. 'Haven't you seen the cockroaches crawling out of it at night?'

I made a face. 'Jimmy Choo sporting pretentious chick can go have her coffee at Barista,' I thought. Why screw our appetites early in the morning? I must have thought that out aloud, because Mayura immediately offered to treat us at the Coffee Day at Spencer Plaza next door. Why not, I thought and signalled to Prathiba that I wanted to go. So the three of us exited the office almost as soon as we'd got in with Shweta joining in, last minute.

'Where are you girls off to?' Matthew-the-idiot called out, just as we managed to get out of the door without Juggu, the nosey accounts director noticing. The four of us collectively shot him our fiercest glare and he respectfully shut his trap and disappeared behind his cubicle.

'So, tell me about your divorce plans,' Mayura said, dripping with sarcasm as she sipped her frappe.

'Ah, here it comes,' I thought. 'There's no such thing as a free frappe.'

'You've got whipped cream on your nose,' I said, trying to steer the conversation away.

'Divorce? What divorce?' Swetha and Prathiba cried out in unison. Too late. The damage was done.

'It's nothing guys,' I said, not knowing what answer to give them. The truth sounded so lame and even if they did believe me, I hated having to burst their happily-ever-after bubble.

'I thought you guys were going to Scotland on your second honeymoon,' Prathiba said in a tone that sounded as if I was breaking up with *her*.

'Yes, to try and work out her hickey-strewn marriage that is falling apart,' Mayura added. I would have poured my cold coffee on the bitch's face, but she already looked like P.C. Sorcar's sidekick with all the make-up and now the whipped cream to boot.

I looked at Swetha and Prathiba's sincere, puzzled faces and promised to talk to them about it later. Mayura chuckled. Swetha shot her a dirty look and I left the table pulling the 'lots of work' card.

No, I didn't thank the clown-face for the coffee.

Back in office, I promised Prathiba and Swetha the real story over lunch and managed to get some work done before 2.30 p.m. – the lunch time we had agreed on. That was the nice thing about Bennet & Cole. Nobody really cared about what time you walked in, walked out, went for lunch or even *if* you went for lunch. But of course, when things went wrong, it was your fault. Always.

We didn't mind that, so we stuck to our routines – walking in and out when we felt like it, shooting paper rockets at each other till six in the evening when work usually began and then blaming the boss for running the place like it were a high-school frat club. It was funny that it had never occurred to anyone how I never complained about the erratic timings. I mean, if I were really happy with Rish, wouldn't I have wanted to get back home early like all the other married people? But then, I suppose they imagined the hickeys were a result of all the absence and pining. Pfff. People can be so naive.

'Ready to leave?' I asked walking over to where the art people sat.

'Almost, give me a minute,' Prathiba called back.

'Sure,' I said and plonked myself at the reception area with a magazine.

About two minutes later, Parvati our receptionist came over to announce that I had visitors.

Curious, I walked out asking Swetha and Prathiba to join me as soon as they were done. I stepped out wondering if it was Rish coming over to give me more bad news about our parents, but nothing would have prepared me for the sight that unleashed itself upon me and my unsuspecting colleagues. It was my mom, mom-in-law and Reshu periamma in her element. Too horrified to say anything, I quietly went over, said hello and asked them the reason for the surprise visit.

'What a nice office, beta!' my mom-in-law said and I thought I heard Parvati snicker from behind her desk. I turned around and noticed Swetha and Prathiba standing just behind me, looking confused.

I introduced them reluctantly and asked the women again, 'Okay, now why are you here?'

'Don't be rude, Deepu,' my mom interrupted, 'we just wanted to see where you work.'

Swetha made a soft hissing sound to indicate she was uncomfortable and wanted to leave, when Reshu periamma decided to include her in the conversation.

'So, are you girls married?' she asked looking at Swetha who was clearly the more attractive one.

'Umm, no aunty,' Swetha answered, accustomed to desi aunties and their intrusive questions.

'What? Not married? How old are you?' she continued.

Prathiba rolled her eyes, one eye for the intrusion and the other for being ignored.

'Okay, that's where I draw the line,' I snapped.

'You can't just walk into my office and start shooting personal questions at my colleagues,' I spat out. 'I still have to work here'.

All the women tch-tched in unison at this, as if I had just announced I was going to have an illegitimate child after an affair with a random stranger I met by some faraway ocean.

'I'm twenty-eight, aunty, and I'm getting married in December,' Swetha lied, putting an end to all the tension.

Reshu periamma looked pleased at this and took it as an invitation to spill more *gyan*.

'And once you get married, have the baby soon, ma,' she continued, even as my eyes threatened to fall out of their sockets.

'Otherwise your parents will have to send you on a second honeymoon like we're sending our Deepu and Rish.' And all three women blushed as if *they* were going on the second honeymoon.

I couldn't believe them. I looked at Prathiba and Swetha who did an impressive job of appearing like this kind of conversation happened every day with everyone's parents.

I suddenly felt a strong sense of sisterhood that very moment. Like I could tell them anything and they would totally *get* me. We said goodbye to the ladies and lied that we had work to do. Once they left, we made a dash for the food court at Spencer Plaza. Once the first bites of sandwich, channa batura and sambhar saadham settled in our tummies, I decided to give them the promised story. They both remained unusually calm as I related the story of my failing marriage and our decision to get divorced, so I asked if anything was the matter.

'But this is like a kindergarten fight, babe,' Prathiba said. 'This calls for a vacation like your folks have rightly decided, not a divorce.'

I couldn't believe I was hearing it.

'Excuse me?' I snapped, looking to Swetha to give me a hand. 'Are you telling me, in three and a half years of marriage, we might have forgotten to consider those possibilities?'

'Does he hit you?' Swetha stepped in.

'No, of course not!' I answered.

'Okay, has he cheated?' Prathiba added.

'No,' I said.

'Have *you* cheated?' Swetha continued.

'No, damn it!' I almost screamed.

'Are those the only reasons for a marriage to fall apart?' I asked, exasperated.

'Pretty much,' Prathiba said.

'At least in India,' Swetha pitched in.

'How about incompatibility?' I asked totally caught off guard by their response.

'Well tell me which two individuals *are* completely compatible,' Prathiba suddenly sounded like a shrink, hellbent on fixing our marriage.

'You know what I mean,' I bit back, 'what about two people who can't converse without arguing, decide on a wall colour without insulting each others' lineage and hate even celebrities who remind them of their partner?'

'Well, that's what marriage counsellors are for,' Prathiba said in her annoying, aunty-like tone.

That was it. I lost my appetite. If the people who supposedly *got* me, reacted this way, I had no clue what to expect of our families. More so now that they seemed completely smitten by each other.

I stared at the brief in my inbox languidly when Rish texted me at 6:20 p.m. – 'Random people at work think we should see a counsellor! Get the feeling this is going to be no easy task.'

'Ditto here. Should we just run away?' I replied.

'Hold on. We'll work out a plan in Scotland,' came his answer.

'Yes we will,' I replied with a sudden resolve.

And the old team was back on the job.

Eight

The 7th of August was round the corner and our lives couldn't have been more out of order. The Old Wives Club (mom, mom-in-law and Reshu Periamma) gave themselves permission to use our apartment like a hotel room, thanks to mom-in-law's spare key. Mid-afternoon kitty parties, brunch with neighbourhood ladies, late night movies (on our new 40" LCD screen) along with other bored women from the apartment building became the norm, and Rish and I made sure we were never home earlier than 11 p.m. Twice, I came very close to throwing them all out of my living room, but Rish and better judgement prevailed.

'If we're going to get them to listen to us, we have to be nice now,' he reasoned.

'Yes, but I feel like I'm gate-crashing at my own party,' I said through gritted teeth, 'not to mention how much they trash up the place.'

'Only a couple of days,' he cajoled, 'and then we'll be out of here.'

'I cannot believe we're actually looking forward to spending two weeks together in the UK,' I fumed.

'We're not,' he reminded me. 'We're looking forward to working out a brilliant plan that will convince them and ensure we never have to be together again,' he smiled.

Sometimes, the man talked sense.

When I woke up the next morning, I was greeted by two more additions to the Old Wives Club – Rimple aunty and Dimple aunty – my mom-in-law's twin sisters who had come all the way from Delhi because they had never seen our apartment. I mean, what was it, the Taj Mahal? I clenched my teeth and greeted them, trying to focus all my energy on packing my bags and jetting off. Rish had made it a ritual to step into the living room just in time to grab his breakfast and leave, so I was left alone to make coffee for the aunty cohort and endure the Rapid Fire round on the hot seat.

'Beta, you've put on weight,' Rimple aunty uttered the first affirming words of the day.

'Any good news?' Dimple aunty butt in.

'Arre Dimpu, no good news yet, that's why we're packing them off to Scotland,' my mother-in-law decided to field the question.

I sipped my coffee in between awkward smiles, but no one seemed to notice my obvious discomfort. I silently cursed Rish for abandoning me with the women. But then, he *had* decided to forego his morning cuppa, for this precise reason – something the South Indian in me, could never do.

'So, what are your plans?' I asked attempting to sound interested and hospitable. 'Are you planning to do any sight-seeing?' Not that there was much to see in Singara Chennai.

'Oh we thought we'd wait for Kitty and Suhana to get here,' my mom-in-law replied, in an annoyingly matter-of-fact style.

Kitty was Dimple aunty's only daughter and though only a couple of years younger than me, everyone treated her like she was three. The girl by herself was all right though, but together with Suhana – her cousin and second spoilt child of Rimple aunty, turned into something of a giggle machine that you couldn't get to stop. I honestly didn't know why I was still surprised, but I was. And annoyed too. Teeth-gritting, hair-tugging annoyed.

'And how exactly is everyone supposed to squeeze in here?' I asked, letting my irritation surface a bit.

'Oh, that's arranged for beta,' my mom-in-law chirped like a sparrow on steroids.

'Yes, your parents are the sweetest, Deepu,' Rimple aunty decided to elucidate.

I raised my eyebrows and mom-in-law plunged into a 30-minute long explanation about how my salt-of-the-earth parents had decided to pay through their nose to find a nice service apartment in Kodambakkam for the Delhi lot. My mouth opened slightly at this point, as I had never known my parents to be extravagant, my entire wasteful life. She continued to gush about their generosity, hospitality and affableness but after she mentioned the service apartment, the dinners at The Park and the Pondicherry plans, all I heard was 'blah da dida lalala'.

This couldn't be. Why were my parents acting like 16-year-olds who had fallen in love?

Actually, make that twelve. My head swimming in thoughts of the parents I no longer knew, I walked into the room to find Rish dressed and hiding behind his laptop.

'Oh it's just you,' he sighed.

'Why are you hiding?' I asked him, irritated for not having done that myself.

'Umm . . . because the loola ladies are out there?' he answered.

I nodded absent-mindedly and he asked me if everything was all right. I gave him the update on our families and was most pleased to note that his eyebrows went up even higher and his jaw dropped even lower than mine.

The day at office was a blur – coffee break, meeting, lunch break, discussion (on Scotland), coffee break, feigned-headache-drama and sign out. I decided not to give a damn about who or what I might find in my own house and kept my focus on packing. Surprisingly, the house was empty when I entered and I took the opportunity to lock the main door, play music, light scented candles and take a long, therapeutic bath with the bathroom door open – something I hadn't done in ages.

I was only two songs down, when Rish texted – 'Open door'. I sighed and got out of the tub reluctantly and promised myself I'd do this every day once we got the divorce sorted and I had a house to myself. Soaking wet and draped in Rish's Shrek 2 towel, I opened the door to find a horrified Rish, standing along with Kitty, Suhana, mom, mom-in-law, Reshu periamma and her very messed-up, firstborn offspring – Karthick. I don't know what I looked like, but I do remember the girls giggling, Karthick shuffling his feet awkwardly, the ladies blushing, Rish looking like he had a whole pumpkin stuck in his throat and Reshu periamma winking obnoxiously as usual, saying, 'Oh! You two had plans, you should have told us!'

And within what seemed like a few nanoseconds, the crowd dispersed – maybe because I stood there the whole time in my Shrek 2 towel and embarrassed them into leaving. Rish walked into the house like a man who had just signed his death warrant. I could tell he was waiting for me to fire the 'Couldn't you have given me some kind of sign?' type questions, which really never have answers. Much to his surprise however, I just walked back to the bathroom, closed the door behind me and sank in the tub.

I must have been in there for about an hour and forty-five minutes, but when I was out, I found my suitcase packed and ready for the flight. I examined the suitcase closely, checking again, if it was mine he had packed. I could hardly believe it. In our two years of marriage, I had never seen a make-up gesture such as this one from Rish. His idea of making up somehow always involved thongs and Absolut. But here before my eyes, was evidence that the man was actually growing up.

The fact that I repacked the whole thing once he fell asleep is another story. I mean, why would a woman carry Mickey and Minnie pyjamas (as opposed to sexy, satin camisoles) to Scotland even if she weren't exactly travelling with her very irresistible lov-ah.

Still, I did appreciate the gesture.

Nine

Our last day in Chennai was nothing short of chaotic – last-minute shopping, packing, buying Mysore pak and kaju katlis by the kilogram for Twinky, trying to fit them in our already overfull suitcases, looking for misplaced chargers, bickering with Vodafone over their ridiculously-high, international-roaming deposit, the works. The time was five minutes past midnight and our flight to London was at 4:00 in the morning. It meant we had to get to the airport by 1:00. Though with Rish, I wasn't expecting to reach before 1:45 or 2:00.

'It's pointless getting there that early,' he started the usual, stalemate argument.

'Fine, then let's endure the Old Wives Club a little longer,' I answered coolly.

'They've been here a whole week now, another hour isn't going to hurt,' he retorted.

'Rish, beta!' my mom-in-law sashayed into the room. 'Here, take these saris for Twinky,' she said, dumping at least four, extremely expensive-looking chiffon saris with elaborate zari work, in his hands.

'Are you kidding me?' Rish snapped at her. 'Can't you see we're not exactly travelling light?'

'We've not seen Twinky ever since she got married,' mom-in-law put on her emotional blackmail tone.

I stifled a giggle that came out like a snort.

'And this is just a small gift from her mother Rimpu and two aunts who can't travel all the way to London, because of arthritis,' she said and stared at him with the I-gave-birth-to-you-fed-you-with-my-butter-chicken-and-raised-you-and-can't-you-do-this-for-me eyes, with two drops of crocodile tears to boot.

I must admit I was a little happy, watching Rish unlock his suitcase, get rid of a couple of books and another couple of T-shirts to fit Twinky's saris through clenched teeth.

'Let's leave,' he said to me abruptly, shut the door and got into his flight clothes.

'But isn't it too early, darling?' I rubbed it in.

'Yes and you are always right. Now can we please get out of here?' he begged.

There was a note of panic and desperation in his tone. I tried not to laugh. He sounded like a child who accidentally fell in the gorilla's cage, during a visit to the zoo.

'Okay,' I said, 'As long as we both agree on who's right.'

It seemed like we were in the room only for about five minutes, but when we got out, we were greeted by the entire family – my parents, his mother, Rimple aunty, Dimple aunty, Reshu periamma, Kitty, Suhana and Reshu periamma's two messed-up offspring – the James Hadley Chase-reading Arvind and the self-proclaimed cool dude, Karthick. While Rish and I stood there wondering if this meant another family get-together where the women got drunk, the men hid behind newspapers and chemistry textbooks and our living room got trashed, my dad decided to shed some light on the situation.

'So, ready to leave?' he asked, and it seemed as if my mother had threatened him into coming.

'Wha . . . what? Where?' Rish stammered.

'Arre, to the airport beta, where else?' my mother-in-law was kind enough to spell it out.

'Oh, no need for that uncle,' Rish tried the I'm-too-polite-to-let-you-do-that strategy, 'it's late and we've already got a call taxi.'

'Oh very good then,' Reshu periamma chimed in, 'now we can all go!'

'And *why* would we *all go* to the *airport*?' I bit every word so hard, I could have drawn blood.

'To send you two off ma, what else,' my mother came to Reshu periamma's rescue.

'Amma, we're just going on vacation,' I said, trying not to lose my cool.

'For two weeks,' Rish added.

'It's not like we're moving to Europe!' I finished.

'Oh lighten up, ma,' my mother said. 'It will be fun.'

I blinked twice. I could have sworn she didn't know that phrase till a week ago. I quickly scanned the room – my dad was now comfortably seated on the sofa, staring at the ceiling, Arvind was buried in a textbook again, Kitty and Suhana seemed to be making fun of Karthick and Karthick was busy flashing his new Scorpion tattoo peeking from below his body-hugging blue T-shirt, running his fingers through his gelled hair and acting like they both couldn't decide who would have him.

Karthick wasn't aware of it of course, but everything about him screamed Small Town Repression. He was raised in Tiruchy and was normal enough till he did an internship at a graphic design studio in Bombay. After that, for some unfathomable reason, he decided to stick out like a circus clown at every family gathering – it was just his way of fitting in with those he considered cool. He really did deserve some credit though, for managing to stick out in *my* family.

'So, we're *all* going?' Rish clarified one last time.

'Yes, beta. There are two cars now, isn't it? What's the problem?' Dimple aunty asked.

'Fine, let's leave then,' I said, losing my patience. There was some obnoxious cheering from the ladies and everyone walked out the door.

Not wanting to get molested by Reshu periamma, Rish decided to get into the car with the cousins and I followed. So we were crammed in my father's ancient Maruti Esteem, while The Old Wives Club, my dad and Arvind, modestly settled for the call taxi – a sparkling, silver Innova. Rish sat in front with Karthick who was our voluntary chauffeur for the night and I was sandwiched between two over-dressed, giggly girls who refused to tell me what the joke was about. Add a whiney Celine Dion screeching through the speakers to that equation, and I couldn't wait to get to the airport.

'Can you please change the station Karthick?' I asked, after 6.22 minutes of enduring the agony.

'Oh, it's a CD,' he corrected.

'Great, now can you please change it?' I said, visibly irritated.

'Umm. Kitty likes Celine Dion,' he answered, winking at her through the rear-view mirror. 'Don't you Kitty?'

To my utter disbelief, Kitty actually blushed and Suhana stifled a giggle.

'Yes, I like Celine Dion, didi,' Kitty sounded sheepish.

For the nth time that week, I couldn't wait to be alone with Rish again.

I sighed in relief on reaching the airport and I must have done it too loudly, because Rish gave me one of his daddy looks. And by that, I don't mean 'Ooh baby, daddy's home' kind of look, but a 'Behave yourself, daddy's watching' type of look. The Old Wives Club stepped out of their silver Innova and made a cackling noise so loud that every pair of eyes at the entrance turned in our direction.

What was so exciting about sending someone off at the airport at 1:00 in the morning was beyond my capacity to fathom. We grabbed our suitcases from the trunk and tried to move to a corner, so we didn't obstruct the flow of traffic, but The Old Wives Club decided to hug us right there and give us their parting instructions.

'Remember what you're going there for,' Reshu periamma winked, 'use the time well.'

I smiled uncomfortably and Rish pretended not to hear, when she grabbed his face and planted a sloppy kiss on his very flushed right cheek.

'Give my love to Twinky, beta,' Rimple aunty requested and teared up at the thought of her poor, little daughter married to the son of a business tycoon in London, deciding between a beautiful countryside mansion in Wales and a Lamborghini Diablo for her birthday.

'I will, aunty,' Rish answered politely. 'Now, we're getting late for check-in!'

'Bye ma, bye dad,' I said, giving my parents the courtesy hug.

'Have you packed enough warm clothes?' my dad enquired in his typical, pragmatic fashion.

'Oh just remember to have fun!' my mother interrupted, making me blink once again. Never in my twenty-eight years had this lady asked me to have fun, so I shook my head in a daze, telling myself once again that it was all going to be over in a matter of seconds.

'Bhaiya, wait!' Suhana called out as we started walking towards the door that would soon part us.

'Let's take a picture for Facebook!' she screamed.

Not wanting to validate the absurdity of it all by arguing about it, we flashed our 32s for the Facebook picture.

'Right. Done. Now, can we leave?' even Rish lost his patience.

We turned to leave, when something caught my eye – Kitty looking adoringly at Karthick and the latter pushing a lock of hair behind her ear. I'm positive my eyes popped out, but since everyone was so irrationally excited about sending us off, no one noticed me. Or *them*.

'Did you notice Kitty and Karthick?' I blurted out just as soon as check-in was done.

'No, why?' Rish asked casually.

'I saw her looking into his eyes like they were pools of melted Belgian chocolate!' I said.

Rish laughed. 'They're just kids!'

'He's a year younger than me,' I shot back. 'How does that make him a kid?'

'Okay, they're not kids, now can we please talk about this later?' he took the irritated husband tone.

'Like rest for a while, go to London, then to Scotland, come up with a freakin' plan, get back, get divorced, later?' he finished.

'FINE. I love you too!' I spat, as I closed my eyes and rested my head on the hard chair in the seating area.

Act | 2:

London

Ten

'**D**ee-pee-ka Sun–Durr,' the pudgy man at immigration attempted to pronounce my name.

'So, you're here on holiday?' he checked.

'Family visit,' I answered, just like Rish and dad had asked me to. About thirty-six-thousand times.

Rish followed soon after and we were out in no time, unlike the many individuals and families that were retained in a separate section for further verification. I was surprised to note that most of these people were Indians. I always imagined it was the Middle-Eastern men who got slotted in the dodgy list by default.

We walked on and collected our baggage, relieved to have reached at last. We had barely slept the whole night and were exhausted to our bones. But completely taken in by the massiveness of Heathrow, we kept walking on like two lost kids in a candy shop. It wasn't until ten minutes later, that we remembered Twinky's instructions to wait by a certain store, the name of which we couldn't recall.

We then spent another twenty minutes bickering about whose fault it was that we didn't remember the name, when as luck would have it, we were right there, standing diagonally opposite to Boots – the chemist's store that Twinky mentioned.

'I'm so sorry I'm late!' Twinky shrieked as she ran towards us and tried to hug us both at the same time.

Her hair was Chinese-straight, she looked even fairer (if that was possible) and within fifteen seconds, I had noticed at least three of the top ten luxury brands on her person. Actually, I could smell one of them.

'Oh that's fine. We were busy looking around, anyway,' Rish answered politely.

'Yeah, this place is massive,' I added, trying to join the family conversation.

'Oh this is so exciting,' Twinky squealed in delight.

'You're finally here! I already know where I want to take *you*!' she said pointing at me. She was perky and shrill – like she was high on Glucon D.

I smiled, not knowing what to say.

'Oh and *you*,' she continued turning to Rish.

'Raja has a whole lot of things planned for you too!' she informed.

'Wow, I can't wait,' Rish said but Twinky completely missed the sarcasm.

'Let's go on and chat in the car,' Twinky said and skipped along as she led the way.

'Raja?' I asked Rish as soon as Twinky was out of earshot.

'Didn't she marry that guy named Earl or King or whatever?' I continued.

'Shut up!' Rish said, but I knew he wanted to laugh.

'Prince is his nickname! Now, shush,' he cautioned as we neared the car – a deep blue, BMW 5 series.

'*This* is the guest car,' Twinky said as we got in. 'Raja said you guys can take it to Scotland. Varghese will take you around.' She pointed to the jovial Indian man in a white chauffeur uniform, sitting at the wheel.

'Wow,' we both said raising our eyebrows and she seemed happy.

The car began moving and I couldn't help but wish I were sitting inside one of those cute red buses instead. Who wanted to be trapped inside a fancy BMW with windows raised, on their first trip to a new country?

'But Twinky,' Rish said, 'I think we'd rather take the train.'

'The train?' Twinky asked contorting her face as if Rish had just suggested we hitch a ride with Onyx's garbage truck.

'Yes, we just thought it would be nice to soak in the local flavour, you know?' I gave Rish a hand.

'Okay, whatever you guys prefer,' Twinky sulked.

'But I can't wait to do some shopping!' I said, hoping to lighten her mood.

'Oh *didi*, you'll go crazy here!' she shrieked as expected. 'You'll need ten whole days to do justice to Oxford Street alone, one of which would be spent in Selfridges, of course!'

I smiled politely and nodded. I had heard of Oxford Street, but not much else. This was my first international trip and given the chaos that preceded it, I hadn't had the time to grab a Time-Out, Lonely Planet or even do a basic Google research.

'Great, so that's settled then,' Rish said looking out the window. 'Can't wait to get on a bed!'

'After you get under the shower!' I said.

Rish sighed. Twinky giggled. I was just glad we were going to sleep soon.

'Welcome to our humble abode,' Twinky said with rehearsed modesty, as we entered the gates of their mansion located in Kensington, one of London's most expensive residential areas.

'Wow,' I said though her house was just as I expected her life to be – boring and reeking of wealth.

Just then, two Golden Retrievers came bounding in, in our direction. I thought it couldn't get more stereotypical than this. Even their names were Jackie and Jimmy. A golden name board with Mehtas written on it in black, hung on the glorious white wall. Rish and I exchanged a knowing look at the sight of this. To us, the name board read a lot like 'Another Indian family rolling in wealth and lacking in originality, resides here.'

At this point, I started playing a guessing game in my head. What would I find on entering? A Persian cat with a diamond studded collar crouched on a white sofa or a uniformed butler à là Sound of Music? I voted for the cat.

On entering, we found the large white sofa as I had predicted, but crouched on it was not an elegant Persian cat, but a very large woman who appeared to be Twinky's mother-in-law. She wore a diamond-studded choker though, so I wasn't completely wrong about the cat.

'Come, come! Welcome to our humble abode!' The Cat gushed in a fake Brit accent as she raised her heavy behind from the sofa to greet us.

'Oh it's a mansion you've got here, aunty,' Rish gave the textbook answer, completely avoiding eye contact with me, for fear of breaking into a laughing fit.

'Oh it's nothing,' The Cat said, gesturing to us to sit down.

'And how are you, Trinkle dahling?' she directed the question at me.

'I'm Deepika, aunty,' I said, wondering just how she had managed to think I had a name like that.

'Oh of course,' she continued in her annoying accent.

'Princess, get them some tea, dahling!' she said to Twinky.

Rish and I could take it no more and made grunting noises in an effort to control the laughing fit we knew was coming very soon.

'Twinky, could you show me the loo?' I called out, getting up from the sofa and following her.

'The cloakroom is right there, beta,' The Cat said pointing east. Rish snorted and feigned a cold.

I spent a good fifteen minutes in the 'cloakroom', checking out the array of beauty products in the cabinet, trying some of them out and checking myself out in the full-length, Victorian style mirror that adorned the wall. I stayed in for as long as it took for the fit to subside and noted to my relief that The Cat was no longer in the living room with Rish when I reappeared. So we sat there, sipping our Earl Greys and nibbling on scones, while more uniformed men who appeared to be pseudo-Brit versions of desi watchmen, carried our suitcases to our room.

'Ah!' Rish moaned, rolling in our unusually soft, fluffy white mattress that I had only read about in fairy-tale books until then.

'I wish *I* had married Prince!' he said.

'You should have,' I answered, 'they might have called you Queen,' I winked.

'Sometimes, you really are funny, you know that?' he said.

'I know,' I said modestly. 'But we need to find a way to keep them off our backs till we figure out a plan of action for the divorce!'

'Can we please worry about that tomorrow?' he begged.

'Oh come *on*!' I said and he pulled me into bed from where I stood.

'Well all right' I said as the mattress touched my skin and enveloped me in its fairy-tale fluffiness. 'We'll worry about it tomorrow.'

He snored in agreement.

Eleven

We went to bed in the evening and slept right through the night. Our Earl Greys arrived at the room by seven in the morning.

'So what's the plan of action?' I yawned, stretched and made my way out of bed.

'Looks like I should ask Raja,' he moaned.

'Raja that,' I laughed.

'London seems to be bringing out your cheesy side,' he said, laughing.

'It also seems to be making you more bearable,' I said.

'Oh this is relativity honey,' he said, 'I'm only bearable against the Prince and Princess backdrop!'

'Makes sense,' I turned my nose at him, 'I'll remember that.'

'Yes, in about half an hour,' he whispered, tackling me back to the bed in a fit of passion, reminiscent of our early days.

'Wait! Let me brush my teeth,' I said, wriggling out.

'Never mind,' he sighed and began dressing.

He *was* unbearable I thought, and I could tell from the thickness in the air around us, that the feeling was mutual. I mean, is fresh breath such a bad thing to have in the morning? Yet Rish and I always bickered about things like this. He accused me of ruining the flow and killing the spontaneity. I argued that it was worth the trouble as it would only make the whole experience more enjoyable. Now, this might seem trivial. Certainly not big enough to qualify for divorce. But imagine about twenty-five different scenarios such as this one on a daily basis and you'll agree that Rish and I may be better off being friends.

I decided to soak my early morning frustration in a tub full of lavender foam, while Rish decided to go down and meet Raja to find out if he had any slots free in his timetable so he could meet me later to plot our mega, convince-the-family divorce. Turned out, the bath did do me good and I was actually looking forward to the shopping date with Twinky.

'I cannot believe that guy,' Rish barged into the room again. I looked up from the black leggings I was trying to roll up.

'He wants to take me to Madame Tussaud's!' he fumed. 'Do I look like a pimply fourteen year old who wants to stand next to a pouting Marilyn Monroe and grin like a baboon while he clicks a picture to put on Facebook?'

I laughed. The picture was truly hilarious.

'Why don't you just tell him?' I suggested.

'Wouldn't be polite,' Rish answered in his usual it's-not-all right-to-say-everything-that-pops-into-your-head way.

'Then suffer darling,' I said, getting into my knee-high red boots that I had bought in Delhi and never got to wear in Chennai.

'I'm off on my shopping date with Twinky,' I said. 'Try and get off in the evening?'

'Yeah maybe I could tell him I'm planning a romantic dinner with you.'

'Ah. We plan the divorce over a candlelit dinner. No one would guess. It's the perfect crime. You're a genius!' I said.

❉ ❉ ❉

'Didi, you *have* to check this out!' Twinky shrieked for the nth time that day, very close to my ear.

Out of politeness, I feigned awe and fascination at the sight of the hideous pair of candy-pink stilettos she was holding up. It had something furry covering the toes, while the rest of the shoe just gaped at me unapologetically in its candy pink sweetness. I wanted to barf, but politely agreed to try it on.

The next thing I knew, Twinky was swiping her credit card to present me with the ugliest pair of shoes I ever set my eyes on.

'No Twinky, I can't let you do that!' I tried to stop her.

'Oh come on didi, enjoy your last pair of high heels,' she said.

'And why is it my last pair?' I asked, shifting my focus from the ugly shoes for the first time.

'Because you can't wear them through your pregnancy, silly!' she giggled.

I blinked.

'That's why you're here na? To make babies?' she giggled some more.

'Right,' I said uncomfortably. 'Which reminds me, I'm meeting Rish for dinner at eight.'

I was suddenly in a desperate hurry to see him and I silently hoped his day had gone just as bad.

'Oooh. Dinner plans. That's always a good start,' Twinky winked.

'Sure is,' I winked back. And felt a sudden rush of hope shoot up my spine, as I pictured Rish and myself making constructive divorce plans over French cuisine and red wine.

Twinky's car dropped me off at Pearl Restaurant and Bar – the Mehta family's pick for special occasions such as this one. Rish and I knew at once that we wouldn't like it, but what better place to come up with an elaborate divorce plan than a fancy French restaurant where you could spend a good four hours savouring a three-course meal over many glasses of expensive, bitter-tasting wine?

I entered what seemed like the Pearly Gates of Heaven. They weren't kidding. Every wall was decorated with hand-strung pearls and the chandeliers did a fine job of making my knee-high red boots feel embarrassingly out of place. I spotted Rish sitting at the corner table looking extremely happy with himself, just as I was about to ask a waitress for help.

It didn't take much conversation to realize that Rish had already sampled three different wines and any hopes I had of coming up with constructive plans had probably crumbled half an hour ago. I stared wistfully at the couple seated by the window. The girl was wearing an elegant blue silk dress that ended below her knees in slits, with a gorgeous ink blue stone pendant that stood out against her perfect golden hair falling right down to her waist. 'Now that's how you dress for this place,' I thought and forgot all about dress code when I noticed her boyfriend looking at her adoringly with his stunning green eyes.

I turned my eyes back to a very inebriated Rish, grinning like a monkey and tried to tell myself that this was no place to break a bottle over his head. But just as I was convincing myself that we would somehow find a way to end this marriage sooner or later, Rish came up with something so brilliant and out of character.

'Let's not try to convince them about us having a bad marriage,' he said. 'Let's just convince them that we're bad children-in-law.'

I pondered this as the waitress poured me a glass of the same red wine Rish was having.

'Makes sense,' I said taking my first sip, 'they don't really care about our happiness anymore, they only care about theirs.'

'Exactly,' Rish smiled his wicked smile as the waitress poured him another glass. 'This is our chance to let our in-laws know exactly what we think of them.'

'That is so bad ass,' I said gulping down my glass of wine as the waitress stared in part horror and part disgust.

'Now I remember why I married you,' I smiled.

By the time we got through our wild salmon with caviar, shrimps and veal, the guy seated by the window had got the waitress to bring the champagne glass with the diamond ring in it and Rish and I were drunk enough to stick our tongues out at them. We could tell the waitress couldn't wait to have us clear the table, but we were too happy.

'So, I just have to tell The Cat that she's a pretentious buffoon and her diamond choker might look better on an actual cat,' I said laughing through a mouthful of cheesecake and strawberries.

'And I will call your people Madrasis and tell Reshu periamma she's a fat, old and ugly version of an 80s Tamil Cinema vamp,' Rish said choking on his wine.

My phone beeped just then. It was a text from Twinky. 'How is it going? Tell me I'm interrupting.'

'Smooth. And yes, you are interrupting,' I replied, winking at my partner in crime.

Twelve

When I woke up the next morning, things didn't seem quite as simple as they did when I was four drinks down. I couldn't just tell my in-laws what I thought of them even if they oozed fake affection, spoke in annoying accents, wore diamond-studded necklaces and thought my name was Trinkle.

We had to come up with a better plan. Maybe I could get Rish to 'accidentally' blurt out stuff about me to his relatives and I would return the favour when we got home? I bounced the idea off Rish who only seemed too keen to get started. After a good two hours of lazing in our fluffy mattresses and another hour soaking in the jacuzzi, we decided to join the family for breakfast. Rish didn't even have to try too hard with Twinky around.

'We didn't expect you guys to be up so early,' Twinky started.

'Yes, neither did we,' Rish answered in his matter-of-fact way.

'Oh you have to see the pair of high heels I got didi!' Twinky said, pulling out the ugly pair of candy-pink stilettos.

'Those?' Rish said, his eyes popping. 'She really picked those? They are hideous and she hates pink!' He looked at me befuddled.

I gulped down my fresh orange juice and tried to make conversation with The Cat. Somehow all of this seemed so simple with wine.

'Still,' I thought, 'Twinky will now know I'm a liar and start disliking me.'

To return the favour, I opened conversation with Raja, not daring to look in Twinky's direction.

'So what did the boys do yesterday?'

'We went to Madame Tussaud's,' Raja answered.'It's a typical tourists thing, but it's a must-see and Rish had a . . .'

'You went to Madame Tussaud's?' I interrupted laughing and choking on my orange juice.

'Rish would have agreed to cross the street in my camisole if it were an alternative!' I said continuing to laugh, unmindful of the others. Now it was Rish's turn to squirm, but I could see the same We're-doing-this-for-a-good-reason conviction take over him, just as it took over me a couple of minutes ago and he broke into a fit of laughter too.

The Mehta family cleared the table one by one and we felt a sense of accomplishment at last.

We went back to our cosy room to laze a little while longer and around noon, there was a knock on the door. Imagining it was The Cat coming to throw us out for bad behaviour at breakfast, I cautiously approached the door. It was Twinky and she wanted to speak with me in private.

'This can't be good,' I thought, but shooting Rish one last look of apprehension, I followed Twinky to the garden.

She waited till we walked up to the gorgeous white swing and perched our butts on it, before she let the floodgates open. I fumbled for words, not knowing what to say, while reassuring myself that this was for the greater good, when Twinky decided to enlighten me on the pointlessness of our plan.

'You hated those stilettos and you still let me buy them for you simply because I loved them so much,' she sobbed.

'Oh my God,' I thought. 'This isn't going where it's supposed to be.'

'You are like the big sister I never had and you're the best,' she continued, oblivious to the horrified expression on my face.

'Ma, Dimple aunty and even Neeti aunty were wrong about you when Rish bhaiya wanted to marry you,' she burst out some more.

'You are nothing like that Tamilian girl who married Babli aunty's son Mintu for his MBA and fancy cars,' she blew into her hanky.

'You love your husband and his family so much, you lie for them,' she finished. 'We're all so glad that you're in the family,' and with that she hugged me like she wouldn't let me go.

After what felt like a never-ending hug and sob session, I made my way up to the room to tell Rish about our plan gone horribly wrong but nothing would have prepared me for what I saw on opening the door – Prince, with his big, strong Punjabi biceps wrapped around a very traumatized-looking Rish.

'At least, the plan backfired uniformly,' I thought and closed the door on the hugging machos.

Thirteen

It was only Day 3 of our stay in London and we couldn't wait to get to Edinburgh already. Initially, the thought of visiting the most romantic country in the world in such a jaded, loveless state seemed unbearable. But now, we just wanted to run away from all the love as fast as we could and remain blissfully cynical, loveless and angry together.

'Maybe we could cut our London trip short and go to Edinburgh' I thought, lazing once again on our wonderful fluff of a mattress, while Rish decided to sleep away the disturbing doses of affection he had received from Raja earlier. I laughed thinking about it and slowly my thoughts drifted to Rish being smothered by Reshu periamma and then, to home.

We hadn't heard from the Old Wives Club ever since we reached and I suddenly wondered if that was good news. I thought about our own apartment back in good old Chennai and tried hard not to imagine the drunk women there but the image would just not go away. I shuddered at the thought of getting back home and dealing with stacks upon stacks of Domino's pizza boxes and empty vodka, whisky and soda bottles.

'Isn't it odd that our folks haven't called since we got here?' Rish asked stretching, as if reading my thoughts.

'Maybe we should call them,' I suggested. There was a knock on the door and in a second, Twinky was inside the room, holding out the phone and looking suspiciously elated. She couldn't speak either, which meant she was delirious with joy. She only ever looked like that when presented with an array of Gucci and Prada merchandise to choose from.

'Maybe someone bought her another fancy car' I thought, grabbing the phone from her hand.

'Hello?' I said into the receiver, not knowing whom to expect at the other end.

'Beta!' It was my mother-in-law's unmistakably chirpy voice. What could she have possibly said to get Twinky this excited?

'Beta!' she shrieked again. 'Our Kitty and your Karthick!'

She had barely uttered the words when I thought I was going to throw up. I handed the phone to Rish and rushed to the bathroom. I couldn't believe it. We had only been away four days and the news had reached the parents? And what were they so excited about in the first place? Kitty and Karthick barely knew each other and this had to be nipped in the bud. And exactly how were we supposed to get divorced if the rest of our family were marrying into each other?

I stared at the mirror long and hard trying to think, when it hit me – nobody ever said anything about Karthick and Kitty getting married. I hadn't even heard the woman out! Maybe she had called to tell us what a terrible idea it was and was probably asking us to talk them out of it.

'It has to be that way,' I told myself, 'it can't be true.'

'It's ridiculous ma!' Rish yelled into the phone, confirming my suspicion that the supposed adults of the family were taking this puppy love too seriously.

'How long do they know each other? Five seconds?' Rish yelled some more, driving a very disappointed Twinky out of the room. I watched in disbelief and listened closely to every line he spoke till he confirmed my worst suspicions – 'They can't get married ma! Don't be crazy!'

And that was when I first thought that perhaps the universe had conspired against our divorce.

'You were right,' Rish said to me softly after hanging up. 'You did see something between Karthick and Kitty that night, after all.'

'Well if it's any consolation, I thought the matter could wait till we returned,' I said.

'They want to get married next month,' Rish bit each word.

I stared listlessly at the walls and tried to process the news in silence.

Outside, Twinky, Prince and The Cat were engrossed in conversation that came to an abrupt halt as I walked in. I excused myself and tried to walk away when The Cat spoke, 'So, tell me about your brother Karthick, Trinkle beta!'

'My name isn't Trinkle, Karthick isn't my brother and I don't know much about him,' I was too mentally drained to bother being polite.

'Oh come on now beta, you wouldn't be jealous that Kitty and Karthick are stealing your thunder now, would you?'

My response was just an expression of genuine bewilderment.

'You know what I mean, dahling,' The Cat continued 'All these years, you and Rish were the ones with the Two States marriage and now you have a younger couple competing with you for the spotlight!'

I couldn't believe her. Thankfully, Twinky came to the rescue. 'You guys just need some time to process it didi,' she said trying to be reasonable.

'Yes we need time,' I said absent-mindedly. 'We definitely need time.'

I went all over the house looking for Rish and when I finally found him on his fours in the garden, playing with the retrievers, the time was already 7:40 in the evening. We had spent a whole day fielding shock after shock and we were still without a plan.

'We need a plan and a good one,' I blurted out.

'Something that doesn't make them ooze love, something that can stop an irrational wedding, something that actually works!' I cried helplessly.

'Let's just go to Edinburgh,' Rish said, wrestling Jackie, the bigger of the two golden retrievers.

'And that's your solution?' I asked exasperated. 'Running away and not facing the situation like you always do?'

'What do you want me to do?' he asked calmly, not taking his eyes off Jackie or the smile off his face.

Something about his calm was odd and irritating and I watched him for a bit in silence.

'You should come here and try this,' he said. 'It's very therapeutic.'

Without a second thought, I dove into the wrestling arena and tackled both Jackie and Rish to the ground.

'Ha!' I gloated.

And for a second it seemed like we were having a moment. Only for a second though, as Twinky had arrived on the scene to remind us what a cute couple we made and that we were the model couple in the family and oh how she wishes Prince would look at her the way Rish looked at me.

We both stifled a giggle at this point, but Twinky continued about marriage and children and how we would make gorgeous, super-smart children and that the Two States marriage was the best thing that happened to both families and oh how happy she is for Kitty for finding a boy from my family and once we get over the initial shock, we're going to be so excited about the next wedding in the family and do I think she should wear her new indigo Satya Paul saree for the wedding or the gold chiffon, and on and on and on.

Thankfully, we were interrupted for dinner. When we had finally made our way inside the mansion once again and got seated at the table, it was Prince's turn to gush.

'You two make a fine couple,' he began as Twinky shook her head in agreement.

I wondered if the Prince and Princess had been instructed by the all-knowing Cat to make us feel better about the younger ones stealing our spotlight.

Rish fidgeted with his fork which was a sign that he was uncomfortable.

'In fact, I wish I had found a South Indian bride,' Prince continued looking for someone to acknowledge his joke, but only Twinky laughed hesitantly.

'Anyway, forget that,' he said, 'Twinky and I were thinking it would be good fun if the four of us went to Edinburgh together.'

Rish dropped his fork on the plate, making a loud, clanging noise and I choked on my paratha in response.

'Oh a double honeymoon,' The Cat squealed, 'I'm jealous.'

I smiled my best fake smile and Rish picked up his fork again.

'Well, what do you think?' Prince asked eagerly.

'Well I think it's a fantastic idea,' Rish said, causing Twinky to cry in happiness and me to choke on my paratha yet again.

'Fantastic idea?' I screamed once we were back in our room.

'What was I supposed to do, I was cornered!' Rish bit back.

'Well, how are we supposed to come up with a plan if they are in our face all the time talking about weddings and babies?' I asked.

'I'm guessing we will have a room of our own where we can make plans?' he answered.

'Oh come on. That never works!' I threw my hands up in frustration.

'Well we need to handle one mess at a time,' Rish said. 'First the wedding, then the divorce.'

'First some sleep after a day gone horribly wrong,' I said, crawling into bed.

'Right,' he answered. 'Tomorrow might just go right.'

Fourteen

The next four days disappeared in a blur, mostly involving ridiculous amounts of pre-nuptial excitement over calls to and from India. Was the wedding going to happen the Punjabi way or the Tamilian way? Will it take place in Chennai or in Delhi? How many ceremonies are there going to be? What will Kitty wear? Does she like lehengas? 'Cause there is this really nice place here, you know? Will they come to London for their honeymoon?

Twinky had enough questions to fill every moment that went without someone saying a word. It was almost as if she was making up for the fact that she lived so far away from her family. There was no other way to explain the frenzy she drove herself into – hanging on the phone, going window shopping for Kitty, buying bridal magazines, doing Google searches through the night and insisting that I stay by her side for every one of said activities because of course, Rish and I were the model couple.

Rish on the other hand, was taken on a massive sight-seeing tour of London by a doting Prince who reminded him every one hour about us being the perfect example of marital bliss. For the nth time since we decided on the divorce, I longed to be with Rish. Especially if it meant getting away from Twinky's high-pitched gushing.

We were leaving for Edinburgh the next morning and the thought was suddenly as frightening as my recurrent nightmare – showing up unprepared for my chemistry exam. I tried to tell myself that it didn't matter who married whom, that we shouldn't really care if the family agreed, we should just go ahead and do what's best for us, for our marriage. My phone rang just then, interrupting my self-pep-talk. It was Reshu periamma. 'No, God,' I thought, 'I don't have the energy for this now,' but I picked it up anyway.

'What if it was an emergency? What if the Old Wives Club had accidentally set our apartment on fire with all their drunken parties?

'Periamma?' I said fearing the worst.

'Deepu!' came the far-from-agitated voice at the other end. 'How is the baby-making coming along?'

'Uhh we're having a good time periamma,' was the best I could come up with. 'How are things there?'

What I really wanted to ask was 'Who's staying where.' Thankfully Reshu periamma was the queen of over-sharing, so I got what I needed to know.

'We oldies are staying at the guest house and what a blast we've been having . . . blah . . . blah . . . the other day we went to Pondicherry and your mother tripped on the road, trying to walk in her new drain-pipe jeans . . . blah . . . blah . . . and the kids are all staying at your place and Karthick is throwing his bachelor party there . . . blah blah blah.'

I didn't know whether to be horrified at the thought of Karthick trashing up our place with cigarette butts, bottles of booze and possibly questionable videos and women, or ask why on earth my mom was wearing drain-pipe jeans. Reshu periamma of course was oblivious to my silence and continued telling me about the family's travel plans, get-togethers, marriage preps, the colour of the neighbour's new car and her suspicions that the man in 2A was having an affair with the lady in 2C when his wife was away at work.

After an hour of listening to Reshu periamma's talk-a-thon replete with shocking, stomach-curdling snippets of information, I decided what I needed was a long uninterrupted bath with scented candles, Lavender soak (to help me relax) and Blackmore's Night playing softly in the background.

I don't know how long I was in there, but when I stepped out and came into the room, still dripping with water and draped in a towel, Rish was sitting on the bed sulking like a five year old and looking very much like he could use a long bath himself. I took a deep breath and braced myself, expecting to hear more bad news from him.

'Can we just tell them?' he broke the silence, 'That we're getting divorced?'

'I'm all for it!' I said. 'What happened?'

'My dad called,' he said finally.

Whatever else I may have foreseen, this I could have never guessed. Rish's dad was a bit of an anti-social character in the family that no one liked to hang around with. Though he never left his wife and son, he was constantly away on 'business' trips that Rish was cocksure had to do with a bungalow and a twenty-something who was after his money.

Obviously, the two were perennially at loggerheads until the day Rish announced he wanted to be with me. Though he shot the idea down initially out of habit, on meeting me once and learning that I was a whisky drinker among other things that we both had in common – including a wry sense of humour, my hard-to-please, people-hating, family-abandoning, pop-in-law, decided I was the best thing to happen to their family and did his very best for us to get together even initially, when the rest of the family was against it. He never kept in touch, but since then, Rish felt a compelling need to not let him down.

'Well, what did he say?' I asked impatiently.

'He said he heard we are going to have a baby and he wanted to apologize for having been such a crappy father figure, but that he was sure that I would make a fantastic parent, because I already am the dream husband.' He spoke at 5000 words per minute.

'I'm sorry,' I said softly. 'Do you want to tell the family already then?'

'No, I think I'll just sit in the jacuzzi now, go to Edinburgh tomorrow, get back home, participate in the wedding and *then* tell them,' he said.

'But wouldn't things get a whole lot more difficult if we didn't stop the wedding?' I asked.

'We can't stop the wedding,' he said in his matter-of-fact tone. 'Just like they can't stop the divorce.'

I just nodded as he stepped into the bathroom and it hit me for the very first time – 'They can't stop the divorce' I said to myself, smiling.

We really didn't have to try so hard to win everyone's approval. This was our life together and we had every right to do what we wanted to with it – especially since there were no children in the picture. No, we were not about to be dictated by our families. The thought was liberating. I already felt better.

Then I lay in bed and looked forward to bagpipes, kilts and whiskey without the 'e'.

Act | 3:

Edinburgh

Fifteen

I was hoping for a quiet six hours on the train to Edinburgh with just the scenic countryside for company. Since Twinky had seemed disgusted with the idea of taking the train, Rish and I had imagined they would follow us in one of their fancy cars. But of course this was us – the dying-to-be-divorced couple whom over-excited relatives could quite literally never leave alone, so the Prince and Princess graciously obliged to travel as mortals did and joined us on the train.

The next six hours were simply an overdose of Punjabiness for me. And surprisingly, for Rish too. I mean, did they really have to eat *all* the time? We had our breakfast back home and we were to reach Edinburgh by two in the afternoon, so a coffee and a snack might have been justifiable. But Twinky had packed chicken sandwiches, chicken kathi rolls, mini samosas, paneer tikka, potato chips or *crisps* as they liked to call it, three different flavours of Tropicana and of course bottled mineral water.

It reminded me of train journeys back home as a child, when we had to spend more than a day on the train. Only difference was, everyone on Howrah mail was doing it. Here on the other hand, people were trying hard not to gawk at us. In their defence, we did appear to be something out of Peter

Sellers' movie *The Party* and it was only their good manners that got in the way of their desperate need to stare. Twinky and Prince were oblivious. Rish thought sitting by the window with his eyes closed and Ipod plugged into his ears would turn the whole thing into some kind of bad dream. Except, Twinky didn't let it be.

'Come on bhaiya, you'll love this,' she insisted, holding a paneer tikka stick to his mouth. Rish succumbed in embarrassment, while Prince pulled the earphones out of his ears.

'Arre, what's the point in travelling together if you're going to be sulking in a corner with your Ipod?'

I gave Rish an I'm-so-enjoying-this look over my copy of *Eat Pray Love*.

'And what are you reading here for?' Twinky decided to follow her husband's genius cue and pulled my book away. Rish appeared satisfied. Prince just found the whole thing very funny.

'Okay, Twinky, give it back to me,' I said, 'I'll just leave a bookmark and put it back inside.'

'Elizabeth is in her thirties, settled in a large house with a husband who wants to start a family. But she doesn't want any of it. A bitter divorce and rebound fling later, Elizabeth emerges . . . .' Twinky read the synopsis from the back of the book and I watched her expression sway from amused to disapproving to why-the-hell-are-you-reading-this.

'Why on earth are you reading this didi?' came the question.

'It's a good book Twinky, she's a very talented writer,' I said trying to remain calm.

'But she clearly has no values,' she screeched. 'And you are happily married and trying to have a baby,' she announced for the entire train to hear.

'What if you get influenced by it?' she suddenly lowered her voice to a whisper as if this was the part no one was supposed to hear.

I didn't know how to react to that, so I tried Rish's diversion technique in situations like this and asked her if she could please pass me the sandwiches. I then told her how much I loved the sandwiches and since Twinky had the attention span of a gold fish, *Eat Pray Love* and Elizabeth Gilbert's value system were quickly forgotten for the rest of the journey.

I looked out the window at the gorgeous green countryside and tried to drown in thoughts other than Punjabi food, Punjabi women and Punjabi values, when my phone rang. It was mom.

I hadn't spoken to her since we reached London and I didn't know if I was relieved to get a break from Twinky or frightened of hearing more news of drain-pipe jeans and bachelor parties.

'Amma!' I said, sounding more excited than I was.

'Deepu!' she gushed back. 'How are you? How is Rish? Are you in Scotland?'

'We're on the way with Twinky and Prince,' I informed. 'What's happening there?'

'Oh lots,' came the prompt reply. I braced myself.

'Kitty is away in Delhi buying her wedding trousseau and Karthick is having an early bachelor party because he wants to have it at your place before you both are back.' I was thanking God that there was nothing in it to give me palpitations when mom opened her mouth again.

'Oh and I fractured my ankle at dance class and can't walk, so the ladies are staying with me at our house,' she added casually as if dance classes, drain-pipe jeans and high heels have always been her kind of thing.

'What?' I said. 'What dance class?'

'Oh nothing to get stressed about Deepu,' she explained, 'We just thought it would be fun to enrol for a Cha Cha class together.'

'Cha Cha?' I repeated. Since when did my ultra-conservative, Carnatic-music-loving, schoolteacher-type mother like to Cha Cha? All ears perked up at this and Rish, Twinky and Prince couldn't wait for me to put the phone down, though Rish appeared more afraid than amused to hear the news.

'So where will dad stay if you ladies hog the place?' I asked getting irritated with my mom for acting like a reckless seventeen year old.

'Oh didn't Rish tell you?' she asked.

'Didn't Rish tell me *what*?' I bit the words, glaring at Rish. He looked confused.

'His father is here and both men seem to get along like a house on fire,' she laughed.

'So they're at the guest house,' she continued. 'You know, his dad has a great sense of humour. He's the one helping with Karthick's bachelor party!'

'His father is there,' I repeated for Rish to hear. Twinky and Prince looked irritatingly happy and Rish's eyes popped out of their sockets.

'What the hell is he doing there?' he whispered to me.

'Why don't you find out yourself,' I whispered back before saying, 'Speak to Rish mom' and thrust the phone in his hands.

That was just all the news I could process over one conversation. And from Rish's responses I could tell that my mom had told him how glad she was to have him for a son-in-law, his mom had asked him to bring chocolates and gushed about how it was our marriage that turned his father into a man, Rimple aunty had asked him to tell Twinky to send back the sarees she didn't like and Reshu periamma had said something that made him turn beet red and go ' Uhh . . . I can't hear you . . . you're breaking up . . . okay bye.'

Rish and I sat in silence for the rest of the journey despite Twinky's persistent questions, suggestions to play cards and spoilt-seven-year-old sulking. Prince decided to make some business phone calls and I continued staring out the window, thinking of Edinburgh and hoping to get drunk enough to find conversations with Twinky and Prince intellectually stimulating, and the thought of my mother in drain-pipe jeans doing the Cha Cha, funny and endearing.

I looked at Rish with his eyes closed and head tilted towards the window. I wondered what was going on in his head and felt genuine empathy for him. Was he thinking about all that his dad had said? Was he struggling with all the guilt? Was he angry with himself? With me? Was he thinking of our marriage just now and how come we managed to get here? I couldn't stop the thoughts pacing through my mind as I watched him.

'Poor Rish,' I thought. 'He probably won't be able to sleep till he meets his dad and gets this over with.'

He snored, shattering my illusions all over again.

Men.

Sixteen

We weren't prepared for the cold that hit us on stepping outside the station in Edinburgh. London was pleasant and as summery as it gets in the UK and all we had on now were wafer-thin excuses for windcheaters. The winds blew so strongly that scarves, caps and stoles flew in different directions. I turned around and found Twinky struggling to get her jacket on – her pint sized body jarring against the backdrop of oversized Scottish people.

I found myself wishing that the winds would carry her and Prince away too, but scolded myself severely for it soon after. We walked on with Prince leading, Rish close at heel, Twinky walking fast to keep up and me, ambling at the end of the line, admiring the buildings, observing the people, savouring the flavour and taking in the experience. I had no clue where we were headed and for a change I enjoyed not knowing.

It was good enough that Twinky's voice wasn't hurting my eardrums at this very moment. I was tired and looked forward to reaching our bed and breakfast and literally shutting the door on the family. We got into a bus and I got myself a window seat and was thankful that the seat next to mine was taken. But the nice old lady who sat next to me got down at the next stop and I had to endure Twinky's complaints about UK's pathetic public transportation for the next ten minutes.

Sometimes Twinky made statements that made me forget the fact that she was born, raised and lived in India till she was well into her twenties. As Twinky droned on about the bad seats, I noticed that Prince and Rish had got seats just before us and Rish was subject to his own share of agony with Prince cracking Santa-Banta jokes for the entire bus ride.

'Please let us reach God,' I prayed. And it was our stop.

'Thank you God,' I said, but God was silent.

We decided to stop by at a restaurant for lunch before hitting the bed and breakfast and I found myself relaxing again. We were going to reach very soon and Twinky and Prince would not be in our face for as long as we pleased.

'We could always pull the baby-making card to keep them out,' I thought with a sinister twinkle in my eyes.

'What are you having?' Rish asked passing me the menu card. We were seated at what appeared to be a bar-cum-restaurant and I scanned the menu quickly before ordering Thai red curry, rice and a glass of orange juice. Rish decided to split the food with me, while Prince went for chicken-mint wraps and Twinky sat by and criticized the quality of the food after trying a spoonful of each.

Rish and I raised our eyebrows at each other and continued eating quietly and Prince having finished his wraps in a jiffy, flipped through the menu and enlightened us on what Haggis, the famous Scottish delicacy was made of and ruined our perfectly good appetites. By the time we left the restaurant and took a cab to our bed and breakfast, it was four in the evening. The B&B was like any other in the locality – small and cosy with flower beds and a perfect roof, like a page out of a fairy-tale book.

I was surprised that the Mehta family had actually consented to staying in anything less than a plush five star hotel, but the place appeared every bit like the Scotland I had pictured in my head, so I thanked God once again, but he was still silent. A tiny man welcomed us inside and took us up the carpeted stairway to show us our rooms. 'Almost there,' I told myself and followed the gang up the stairs. The next thing I saw was Twinky and Rish staring with open mouths at the opened room and Prince saying, 'It's all we could get in the last minute, with the Edinburgh festival going on.'

'This can't be good,' I thought as I walked up to them, picturing roaches on the floor, but what I saw was worse than that. It was a twin room, which normally meant a room with two single beds. Except in this case, it was a room with two bunker beds.

'You can't be serious!' Rish blurted out quite out of character.

'Come on people, it's just three nights,' Prince cajoled.

Twinky made a small whimpering sound and I continued staring with my mouth open.

God chuckled.

We decided that staying in wouldn't be a good idea after all and left the room as soon as we had all freshened up. The festival was nothing short of spectacular – the city was a starburst of colours with a line-up of street shows including magic, stunts, stand-up comedy, musicals, mimes and the most extravagant display of dance and theatrical performances.

Once lost in the brilliance of it all, Twinky, Prince and the room we were about to share with them for the following nights was quickly forgotten. Until of course Twinky chose to remind us of her existence by refusing to park her butt on the roads for the street shows or complaining that this was no fun compared to shopping.

I silently vowed to get very drunk before hitting the sack that night. At around eight in the evening, Twinky needed to go to the loo and Prince had to accompany her. We were asked to remain in the same spot until they got back and Rish and I exchanged a meaningful look. The moment they were out of sight, we disappeared from the scene with nothing but escape on our minds. After a good ten minutes of running, we decided to take refuge in a dingy little pub that had really loud live music. It had stone-like benches and smelled of dampness – the kind of place that Twinky wouldn't dream of entering even if she were caught in a blizzard and this was the only place of shelter nearby.

'I cannot believe we're finally alone!' I said to Rish over the music.

'I cannot believe you just said that!' Rish called back laughing. We found ourselves a corner and Rish went to get the drinks as I settled in.

'What are you having?' he asked me using sign language from the counter.

'JD and coke,' I yelled just as the music stopped and everyone heard what I was having. Rish got back in no time with my JD and his rum and I couldn't wait to drown in it.

'To stolen moments,' I said raising my glass.

'And many more to come in the next four days,' he added with a wink.

Four hours and twenty-two missed calls later, we found ourselves outside the pub. And while we didn't feel completely drunk, we also didn't feel the need for our windcheaters when everyone else on the streets seemed to be clinging on to theirs for dear life. I had little recollection of what happened in those four hours, except that there was a lot of drinking and a lot of pointless banter about the people seated by the window, a discussion on how French kissing came to be known as French kissing, a lot of laughter and one broken glass.

As we walked on in the hope of finding a cab, we realized we didn't know the name of the B&B we were staying in and neither of us wanted to call Prince or Twinky. So we walked on until our inebriated feet could take it no more and the cold slowly began biting into us as it did the mortals who wisely had their leather jackets on. Finally, Rish agreed to call Prince. To my surprise the conversation ended rather abruptly and Rish was laughing instead of profusely apologizing for our bad behaviour.

Turned out, Twinky wanted to head back to the B&B and sleep the night off, so Prince dropped her at the room and got drunk all by himself at the pub just next to ours. As Rish related the whole episode to me through peals of laughter, Prince came staggering from the opposite direction, waving at us like an excited five year old. Many hi-fives and wife-jokes later, we made our way to the B&B, Prince supported by Rish and myself on either side.

'Wait till Twinky sees this,' I whispered to Rish, snorting.

'She'll divorce me,' Prince said with a drunken drawl.

'Shhh,' Rish cautioned as we entered.

'What shhhh?' Prince continued. 'This whole happily-married thing is a farce,' he laughed. 'Don't you agree Rish?'

Rish remained quiet.

'You're silent because your wife is here, ha ha haaaaa,' Prince continued.

'That's right Prince,' Rish said, 'I'm afraid she might divorce me,' he made eyes at me as he helped him get on to the lower half of the bunker bed that Twinky was pretending to be asleep in.

'Good night,' I said to Rish smiling at the thought of how the evening went.

'Good night,' he whispered back and pecked me hard on the cheek, rather spontaneously. We locked eyes for just a moment before getting into bed.

'Hmmmmm!' I said tucking myself under the quilt.

'Hmmmmm,' he acknowledged from the bed above.

Seventeen

'I got you something,' Twinky said handing me a box packed in pink glitter with a blue ribbon tied around it. It was about eight in the morning and we were all at breakfast downstairs.

'I meant to give it to you as soon as you reached London, but I thought this was better timing,' she added.

Rish and Prince exchanged curious looks over the breakfast table and I began clawing my way at the box, hoping and praying it was not another hideous pair of shoes. What I found inside appeared to be the ultimate baby-making-essentials kit replete with chocolates (aphrodisiac), lingerie, a '100 favourite romantic ballads' CD, body lotion, massage oil, an ovulation predictor kit and some other unmentionables.

I tried to say something but the words got stuck in my throat. Rish watched the whole drama in quiet amusement, enjoying his bacon and eggs. Prince for once looked embarrassed by one of Twinky's gestures.

I finally swallowed hard and said, 'Thank you.'

'Isn't it great?' she whispered in excitement as if we were the only two people at the table. Or the room for that matter.

'I've got myself a kit too,' she added.

It was now Prince's turn to swallow hard. The rest of the meal happened in uncomfortable silence and I could tell all four of us just wanted to get on with the day.

'So, wanna make babies?' Rish said pulling me out of a crowd that had quickly surrounded a couple of guys juggling torches and swinging from ladders.

'Would this be you flirting with me?' I asked him.

'No, this would be me pretending to flirt with you just so we can get away from them.'

'The honesty is touching, Rishab Khanna,' I called out as I walked on ahead to a souvenir shop.

'Not to mention, incredibly romantic!'

'Well, I wouldn't want to lead you on and break your heart, you know?' he called right back.

I bought a whole lot of magnets, shot glasses and Lochness monster stuffed toys at the souvenir shop for the people at work and a teddy bear playing the bagpipe as a souvenir for myself. As I stood at the counter paying for my stuff, I saw a lady dressed in a flowing rust-coloured skirt, a thin white blouse with long sleeves and three layers of beads hanging from her neck. Her hair was a bright orange which was striking against her pale white skin and hung loose below her waist. She carried a toad in her hand and despite her clothing and the ugly toad, I couldn't help but follow her to wherever it was that she was going.

There was a serene calm about her countenance that made her attractive in an unusual way and with a quick glance behind me to check where Rish was, I continued following the beautiful mysterious lady with the toad. After what seemed like a few seconds of walking, the lady reached an ancient bungalow with a large, mahogany door that had Aura Ville written on it.

She held the door open for me as if she knew I was following all along. What awaited behind the mahogany door though was more of a designer mansion than a dirty, old bungalow with cobwebs and coffins. I tried to hold my jaw from falling as I walked past the swanky furniture and fancy lighting.

The lady walked on to another room, gesturing to me to wait in the living room and I took the time to absorb every detail of this peculiar place – a copy of *Vogue* lay opened on the couch, a Chanel handbag hung from a stand along with a chic suede coat and glittery Venetian masks adorned the bright, fuschia pink wall to my right.

'Not bad for a lady who walks around carrying a toad,' I thought and just then, she stepped out of the room, holding a cigar in hand and looking like something out of *Vogue* herself. I tried to act like everything about her and her mansion was perfectly normal, but she sensed my obvious discomfort.

'It's all right,' she said. 'It's all right to feel disoriented. My name is Irene Walters.' She held out her hand.

That's it? Irene Walters? I thought she'd at least come up with a name like Lady Bazookah or something.

'Deepika Sundar,' I said, shaking her hand.

'Do you know why you're here Deepika?' she asked me, sitting cross-legged on her chair.

'No,' I answered truthfully.

'It's because you're looking for answers,' she said, blowing out a mouthful of cigar smoke.

'Maybe I am,' I admitted, more to myself than to the seriously messed-up stranger.

'Well I'm listening,' she said fixing me a glass of her 27-year Laphroaig Scotch Whiskey.

'No, thanks for your help,' I said, changing my mind. 'But I can't talk about it.'

'Well, fine then,' she said, 'talk about something else' and she handed me my glass.

I must have had it faster than I should have, because within the next twenty minutes, I had told this crazy lady all about our divorce plans and how our families were making it impossible for us to do anything about it.

'Mahvellous deah,' she clapped as if I had just recounted my visit to the moon. 'Nothing like a divorce to make you feel younger.'

'I don't need to feel younger,' I said, 'I just need the families to get out of our way.'

She was beginning to annoy me and I needed to get out before dark, if I wanted to find my way back to the city square where the rest of them were. As I was talking, I noticed the crazy lady staring at her fuschia wall in silence. Just as I tried to enquire if she was all right, she got up and walked away into the room inside. When she returned, she had a large book in her hand which she caressed as if it were a Chihuahua.

'Do you know what this is?' she asked me.

'A very large address book?' I said, feeling stupid even as I said it.

'Bingo! It's my little black book,' she said, 'well not so little.' She smiled.

I peered at it wondering what it was doing in her hands at that very moment.

'Do you want some numbers?' she winked.

'Huh? How is that supposed to help me?' I said. This whole thing was a bad idea. You don't just follow strange toad-carrying ladies into their designer mansions and allow them to peek into your wounded soul over Scotch.

'I'll give you just one,' she said ignoring me. 'Joshua Tebbutt. He'll cause so much chaos in your marriage in twenty-four hours, your families will gladly have you two divorced,' she said coolly.

I got up to leave. The woman was plain absurd.

'Never mind. Thanks for everything,' I muttered and picked up my things to leave.

'Wait!' she called out and I noticed her having a conversation with her wall again. Whatever this was, I didn't have the time for it.

'My point is,' she said calmly as I started out, 'there are a thousand different ways to get a divorce, but you won't get it until you really want it.'

I stopped in my tracks. 'I really want it!' I yelled back with my back still facing her.

'Close your eyes,' she said.

'Why?' I asked. 'Are you a mind-reader? A witch?'

'No, I'm a failed psychotherapist and I'm experimenting on you all over again. Now close your eyes,' she ordered.

I closed my eyes.

'Who is the first person you want to tell this story to,' she asked. 'This whole The-strangest-thing-happened-to-me-today story?'

I blinked.

'Who do you need to be around you when you're extremely happy, agitated or sad?' she asked 'Who is your calmer?'

I kept silent for a while and opened my mouth to answer.

'You can go now,' she said. 'My job's done.'

'Who *are* you?' I asked her turning around.

'I told you,' she said smiling wickedly, 'a failed psychotherapist.'

'No, really,' I insisted.

'Well I really am a failed therapist, because I never quite believed in conventional medicine alone. I can see colours, sense vibrations and hear voices,' she said.

'Umm, doesn't hearing voices make you a patient?' I asked.

'Any genuine psychotherapist worth her degrees will hear voices and if she's really good, her voice will become the voice of wisdom in her client's head as well.'

'What a nut job,' I thought but I couldn't help warming up to her.

'Well, what does a failed psychotherapist charge for her services?' I finally asked her.

'Honest communication between the soon-to-be happily divorced couple,' she winked.

I wanted to get out of there quickly. The woman was sweet and friendly, but she had a way of creeping me out. As if there was something she knew about me and wasn't telling me. I wanted to ask her about the frog, but realized nothing about her made any sense anyway.

'Buh-bye psycho shrink,' I said and she waved back from her chair.

It had been two hours when I stepped out of Aura Ville and I frantically dug out my phone from the bottom of my handbag, expecting panic texts and missed calls but I found none. Puzzled, I put the phone back inside and ran to the city square as fast as my feet would take me. When I finally spotted the three, they seemed panic-stricken for a reason that had nothing to do with me disappearing. For a whole two hours. In a strange land. All by myself.

'What's going on?' I asked and they all looked too caught up in their own clouds of thought to answer.

'Your cousin Arvind swallowed mothballs,' Twinky finally blurted out after I screamed for someone to give me an explanation.

'Intentionally,' Prince added.

'He attempted suicide and is now in the hospital,' Rish clarified, seeing how I still had a blank expression on my face.

My immediate thoughts were of Reshu periamma and how I didn't blame the kid for trying to check out of life this early. Then I scolded myself for thinking that before moving onto the Old Wives Club and all the drama they must be adding to this horrible situation.

'The point is, they need us to get there as soon as possible,' Rish explained.

'Umm, of course,' I said, still dazed.

'They want Rish bhaiya to talk to him,' Twinky said. 'Apparently it had something to do with your aunts and uncles saying he should get into IIT and turn out fine and educated like Rish,' she continued as we walked on.

I swallowed hard. This was all too much to digest.

'Couldn't our families go a day without drama,' I thought to myself and out of the blue, in the dark, Rish grabbed my hand like a frightened six year old.

'I don't know what I'm going to say to him,' he said.

'You can't panic,' I said, 'you're their calmer,' and squeezed his hand.

He squeezed back.

Eighteen

Our highland tour of Scotland was cancelled and the rest of the time we spent there, mostly involved vacant staring into space and monosyllabic conversations. The incident had somehow managed to put Twinky on mute and in a dark, selfish kind of way, I was thankful.

Our train to London wasn't until the afternoon of the following day and since Rish insisted on sulking in the room all by himself, I decided to go sulk with him. The Prince and Princess left to visit the Edinburgh castle and we spent the entire morning sitting on the top of the bunker bed in silence.

I fiddled with the baby-making kit Twinky had given me and Rish played games on his phone. After a good three hours of sulking, we kind of forgot what it was that we were sulking about. It couldn't be because we had to cut our trip short, because all we wanted to do was get away from Twinky and Prince, it couldn't even be Arvind, because he was all right now and Rish just had to have a normal heart-to-heart with him.

'I'm sorry this divorce thing is taking forever,' Rish finally said.

'Don't be ridiculous,' I said, 'It's not your fault that my cousin decided to swallow mothballs!'

'Let's just go ahead with our plans and tell the family later,' he said. 'I can't go back there and face my dad.'

'Ah, that's the problem,' I thought. 'How could I have missed it.'

'If it helps,' I said, 'your dad wasn't entirely wrong.'

'Huh?' he blinked.

'I mean, I'm sure you'd make a fabulous father,' I said.

He looked at me like he thought I had gone crazy.

'And you might even be the dream husband,' I continued, 'if you only realized I'm the better writer between the two of us.'

'That's it?' he mocked, 'You're divorcing me because I want to be a writer?'

'Of course not, that would be silly. It's because you snore.'

Our return journey was as uneventful as six hours with Twinky and Prince could possibly be. We played Rummy, Trump, Literature and on Rish's insistence Scrabble, where the game was only between Rish and me. Prince played words like 'Dot' and 'Pig' that ensured he hadn't crossed fifty points when Rish and I were well over hundred and fifty, and Twinky avoided all double-word scores because she did not like the colour. So after an hour and a half of intense, cut-throat Scrabble war, Rish beat me by three points.

'Winning is about strategy as much as it is about choice of words,' he gloated.

'And that's precisely why I think you're not meant to be a writer,' I said.

He remained silent.

To me, writing was an art form. It was as much about beauty, form and style as it was about content. But Rish could never get that. For him, the story was everything.

'If the story is good and the language simple, people will read,' he often said.

But my point wasn't about people reading as much as it was about creating art. He argued that if I wanted to create art I should paint or write poetry, making me want to shoot him

• **101** •

down for landing on my turf and lecturing me on what I was obviously better equipped to do.

'I'm going to make India read,' he finally announced getting up from his seat with a dreamy look, as if he were The Mahatma and he had just made up his mind about ahimsa.

'Drama King,' I said.'You'd do so much better in Bollywood.'

'Yes, maybe I should make a movie about the fateful day I married you,' he said, taking his seat again.

'You could call it Two Idiots,' I grinned.

'You guys are so cute even when you fight!' Twinky shrieked, startling us both. We had completely forgotten about the existence of our two travel companions since the Scrabble war had begun. I turned around and found Prince asleep by the window.

'Oh we were just discussing your bhaiya's plans of quitting his lucrative, IIT-studded career for a sure-to-fail one in writing,' I said, waiting for Twinky to take over the nagging baton from me and do it justice.

'What? Writing?' Twinky seemed excited. 'Wow, bhaiya that's so awesome!' she hugged him.

Rish was as surprised as I was.

'Well, it's all thanks to Deepika for telling you,' he said rubbing my nose in it. 'Now I think I'll just tell the rest of the family!'

I rolled my eyes and stuck my tongue out at him as Twinky kept hugging him.

He responded with a snort and some thumb-twiddling.

Nineteen

When we reached London, Rish and I were ready to roll into bed and stay there for however long it took to get over all that we had been through since Scotland – Rish's dad's call, my mother's drain-pipe jeans, dance class and fractured ankle, Karthick's bachelor party at our apartment, Arvind's mothballs incident, Twinky's baby-making kit, my strange encounter with the failed psychotherapist and the whole divorce plan that was still nowhere close to execution.

Our tickets to Chennai were rebooked for the day after though, and we had no choice but to get over ourselves, pack and make it to the airport in a day.

'Prince, Princess, Rish!' The Cat called as we entered the mansion, hugging us all in order of affection.

'Trinkle!' she said embracing and kissing me the Page 3 way – where your lips only kiss the air – and I didn't bother correcting her.

'How was Scotland, dahling?'

I didn't know if the question was addressed to me, because she kept looking at Twinky, and Prince and Rish had walked away.

'It was great,' I answered hesitantly, not sure if I had answered out of turn and offended The Cat.

'We had to cut the trip short and we didn't get to do the highland tour,' Twinky sulked.

'Oh right, I'm sorry, I heard about your brother,' The Cat said to me, looking anything but sorry.

'Thanks, he's my cousin,' I said.

'These Punjabis would simply never learn the difference between siblings and cousins,' I thought.

'Oh it's all the same dahling,' she said and called out to everyone.

'Well, tidy up and get ready for dinner, children!' and Prince – the full-grown, married son of a renowned business tycoon, now in charge of his father's business, ran like a puppy to wash up at The Cat's command.

I grit my teeth through dinner and Rish put on his I-don't-find-this-even-remotely-odd face as The Cat tenderly queried Prince about his oral hygiene and his 'bad dream problem'. Justifiably embarrassed, but too much of a chicken to stand up to his mom, Prince excused himself saying he had an early conference call and left dinner halfway. And just when I thought the weird conversations had ended and I could eat peacefully, The Cat shifted her attention to Twinky.

'You must be ovulating now, right Princess?' she asked, taking a spoonful of her leafy salad.

Rish choked on his Chicken Tikka and I was blatantly staring at The Cat.

'Oh yes aunty,' Twinky answered as if this was a perfectly normal and appropriate conversation between a mother-in-law and daughter-in-law. At the dinner table. With guests around.

I had to gape at Twinky now.

'Did you take the pack to Scotland?' The Cat enquired and I gaped some more, speechless.

I couldn't make up my mind about who was worse – Reshu periamma or the mother- and daughter-in-law duo at the table.

'Yes, but I didn't get a chance to use it,' Twinky sulked. 'Perhaps tonight,' she said brightening up.

At this point, Rish started humming a really fast version of the *Godfather* tune, which was his unconscious way of tuning out of uncomfortable situations. He even had different tunes to indicate his level of discomfort. *The Good, The Bad and The Ugly* was for mildly uncomfortable situations, James Bond for medium discomfort, The *Godfather* for serious discomfort and *Mission Impossible* for extremely painful, embarrassing or well, impossible situations. I had only heard *Mission Impossible* when Reshu periamma was around though.

'What about you two, Twinkle dahling?' The Cat turned to me, 'Twinky mentioned you two were trying too.'

'Uh . . . yes we are,' I said softly and turned my full attention to my plate.

'Aunty and I went together to pick the kits,' Twinky explained rather fondly.

'Did bhaiya like the lingerie?' she asked as if Rish were invisible.

'Uhhhh,' I started, but Rish had started humming *Mission Impossible* loudly by then and I broke out into an uncontrollable giggle fest.

Initially, Twinky and The Cat tried to join in the laughter too, thinking I would stop at some point and explain, but they had to give up and leave the table with Rish still humming furiously and me stretched on the floor, laughing and holding my stomach as if my insides would fall out.

It was my best five minutes in London.

Twenty

'I'm heading back to work the day we set foot in Chennai,' I said as we packed the next day.

'Oh but we still have a couple of days,' Rish said. 'We cut our trip short, remember?'

'And I would totally want to spend the extra time participating in all the family joy and wedding hungama,' I said.

'Well we could use the time to see a lawyer,' Rish said making me look up from my bag.

'Sure,' I answered. 'We could.'

'So we're not saying anything to anyone until the wedding is over?' I asked after a few minutes.

'I suppose not,' he said.

'So we live in the same house, party with the same families and basically act like husband and wife?' I asked, talking to myself more than him.

'Pretty much what we're doing now,' he retorted.

'Pretty much what the Prince and Princess, my mom and dad, Brad Pitt and Angelina Jolie and every other couple on the planet are doing too,' I said, mildly offended.

'Except they have sex,' he came up with his only come back.

'Seriously?' I asked him in disbelief, 'is *that* what you're going to tell the lawyer?'

'It *does* make a good argument,' he smiled his signature smile, flashing his dimples.

'Is that all you can think about?' I asked in exasperation.

'Pretty much, when I'm deprived,' he smiled.

I continued packing my bag in silence.

'So, are you packing that little gift Twinky gave you?' he winked.

'Rishab Khanna!' I cried, 'You are incorrigible.'

He laughed.

'And the answer is yes!' I added, still screaming.

'Take care Trinky deah,' The Cat gushed in her fake accent as she hugged us goodbye. I could tell that she resented me for more reasons than being a Tamilian now. I considered for a second if I should apologize for my improp*ah* behaviour the night before, but decided it would be pointless since we were getting divorced.

'Thanks for the hospitality aunty,' Rish said, oozing his share of false politeness.

Twinky and Prince decided to accompany us to the airport and the journey was predictably filled with Twinky whining about how she wished she could go with us and be a part of all the wedding preps, how much she was going to miss us, how sad it was that we couldn't do Scotland justice, how Rish should consider his writing career seriously and how I should use the ovulation predictor kit and get up to speed with the baby-making process.

Prince remained silent as husbands of women like Twinky, my mom and Reshu periamma often did, and I continued telling myself that I could endure a few more minutes of Twinky without breaking down, especially after all these days of rigorous, on-field training.

The moment finally arrived and we did the traditional kiss-hug-and-keep-holding-till-it-gets-awkward thing before finally saying goodbye, promising to add them on Facebook and parting ways.

'You know, I think I see your point,' Rish said as we sat in the waiting area of the airport. 'My family *is* seriously obnoxious.'

'Oh please, I have the mothballs incident on my side,' I said. 'You can't take the Obnoxious Trophy away from us.'

We still had a good hour to go before we boarded and we were both too mentally depleted to read, so we bought ourselves coffee and stretched on the seats.

'But I have The Cat, The Prince and The Princess,' he said, 'and they discuss their oral hygiene, ovulation dates and use cloakrooms.'

I laughed, 'What about having a mom who wears drain-pipe jeans and does the Cha Cha?' I said.

He chuckled. 'Along with *my* mom, you mean. And don't forget my estranged father hiding a young mistress in a bungalow.'

'You don't know that,' I said, 'and besides, I have Reshu periamma,' I said with finality. 'Case rested.'

We laughed, spilled coffee and agreed it was a tie-breaker.

Act│4:
Chennai

Twenty-One

When we landed in Chennai, the welcome we got outdid the one the politician travelling with us received. Though he got garlands and a whole crew of men clad in white dhotis, we had a wedding band (courtesy Karthick and friends) singing 'Lejayenge lejayenge dilwale dulhaniya lejayenge' making everyone at the entrance gawk at us, confetti blasts that I was sure gave the politician a complex, and as I scanned the crowd I even noticed new additions to the cast – Chandu uncle – Rimple aunty's husband and Twinky and Suhana's father, Mohan uncle, our very close family friend and his wife Janani aunty, Tuhin, another one of Rish's cousins who was doing his engineering in Chennai, Shruti, another twenty-something girl whom I only met at weddings and knew I was related to in some roundabout way and finally, Raju uncle, the father of the bride.

We were both pleased to note though, that Reshu periamma was not part of the wedding circus. We graciously grinned our way through it all and walked to the car, escorted by mom and dad who seemed to be in a hurry to kidnap us from the rest of the crowd.

'How was the trip, Deepu?' mom asked, still limping from the fractured ankle and I could tell she wanted to say something.

'It was all okay, ma,' I cut her short. 'How is Arvind?'

'Oh good you asked,' she said gasping. 'We are all so worried.'

I wanted to ask her why the hell there was a wedding circus being staged when everyone's 'so worried' but refrained. Dad and Rish wisely kept out of the conversation and focussed on loading our bags into the trunk of the car instead. The cousins continued with their celebration and decided to hang out at the bar at the airport and the oldies took the other cab and drove home.

'So where is he now, aunty?' Rish asked like a dutiful son-in-law with the added pressure of stacking up to the 'fine and educated boy' title that my family had recently anointed him with.

'He's at our house and poor Reshu's so worried,' mom said. 'She's not been herself at all lately.'

'That's not such a bad thing,' I said, rolling my eyes in the dark.

'What a thing to say Deepu,' came the quick rebuke from mom, but I heard Rish snort and even caught dad quietly enjoying my inappropriate comment in the rear-view mirror.

As we entered my parents' apartment, wide open as usual, I could tell Rish was a nervous wreck. What was he supposed to say to him? That he didn't blame him for feeling suicidal given that he had Reshu periamma for a mom? Or that IIT was a piece of cake and he was sure he'd make it?

'You don't have to talk to him if you don't want to,' I told Rish softly as we entered the living room. Rish's parents, Rimple aunty and Chandu uncle, Dimple aunty and Raju uncle had all reached before us and were seated in the living room, sober and behaving themselves.

'No, that won't be nice,' he said turning to go into the bedroom where Reshu periamma and Arvind were, 'I'll find something to say.'

When Rish entered the room, Reshu periamma stepped out politely, which was quite out of character for her. Also, she did not say or do anything to Rish that made him turn deep pink or hum *Mission Impossible*.

Outside the room, the uncles and aunties discussed the outcome of the IIT-alumnus-to-aspiring-IIT-student conversation that was taking place inside.

'He's a good boy,' my mother said consolingly, patting Reshu periamma's shoulder.

'He will make it into IIT,' she said, as if goodness was the basis on which students were admitted into IIT.

I opened my mouth to say something, but decided it was more fun listening to the conversation.

'He's always studying,' Reshu periamma said oblivious to the James Hadley Chase perennially tucked inside Arvind's chemistry book.

'I don't know why he's so afraid of not making it.'

'Oh don't worry,' Rish's father spoke up, 'I don't remember thinking Rish would ever make it, but he did! And he barely studied!'

'That's because you were barely home to see how brilliant our son was!' my mother-in-law bit back like a Doberman, making everyone in the room uncomfortable.

'He just needs to feel confident,' Mohan uncle said, breaking the awkward silence.

'Yes, just keep encouraging him,' Janani aunty joined her husband.

After what seemed like thirty minutes or more, Rish finally emerged from the room with the happy news: 'He does not want to get into IIT.'

A collective gasp swept through the living room and as everyone tried to come up with something coherent to say, Rish continued, 'He wants to become a veterinary doctor.'

'What?' Reshu periamma asked in a dramatic fashion, with her hand to her chest, 'He wants to become an animal doctor?'

'Uhh, yes?' Rish answered.

'But that's not even a proper doctor!' Mohan uncle and my mom chimed together.

'What do you mean by *proper* doctor?' Rish asked looking visibly put off, 'It's what he wants to do!'

'So what do we do now?' my mother asked looking around frantically and everyone, especially Rish's family remained silent.

'You will encourage him!' I said finally, unable to handle the absurdity.

'Encourage my little boy to become an animal doctor?' Reshu periamma asked sniffing into her handkerchief, as if I had just suggested that he open a brothel or pedal drugs for a living.

'All the men in our family are engineers, architects or managers in big companies,' Reshu periamma continued.

'But my son will sit at a clinic and advise people on what brand of dog food to buy?' she sniffed some more.

'What did you tell him?' Rish's mother asked.

'I said it was wonderful that he cared about animals and felt so strongly about what he wanted to do!' Rish said unapologetically.

'What?' everyone in the room sang in unison.

'What is wrong with you people?' I finally said standing up, not being able to take another second of their drama.

'Rish did the right thing and you better follow suit if you don't want another mothballs incident!'

Rish shot me a look of gratitude from across the room and the oldies murmured among themselves before deciding that we had a point.

When the drama finally subsided and the family was back to its painfully happy, pre-nuptial mood, Rish and I said goodbye to everyone and got ready to go home.

'To the perfect couple,' Rimple aunty uttered the corny words of the day, raising her glass of Rooh Afza to us and everyone cheered as we waved and made our way out.

'And we just set the perfect *backdrop* for the perfect divorce,' I observed as we got in the car.

'We rock,' Rish answered, turning the ignition.

Twenty-Two

We braced ourselves as we opened the door to our apartment, mentally prepared to be greeted by the combined aroma of beer, cigarette smoke and left-over pizza, locked in an apartment overnight. It was supposed to have been Karthick's bachelor party the night before and we had little say in the choice of venue, let alone the guest list, code of conduct or food menu. My stomach churned as I pictured my *cool* cousin Karthick's *cool* friends doing a bunch of *cool* things in my living room.

'Here it comes!' Rish said, letting us in.

I blinked as I switched on the light. The living room was immaculate. There was no stench of cigarettes, beer or left-over pizza. In fact, the house smelled divine, as if someone had broken a bottle of perfume. We both walked on, sniffing the air, to see where the trail would lead us.

'Candles!' Rish called out from the bed room, 'and satin, and . . .' he gasped.

I had to enter the room to see what he meant. Our bedroom had somehow transformed into one of those first-night suites, except this did not have rose petals arranged in a tacky, heart shape on the bed. Instead, there were candles – hundreds upon hundreds, from the seriously huge ones to the cute, miniature ones, red and white and silver, green and gold and ochre, carved and simple, with scents fusing into one another, on the window sills, hanging from lamp stands, around the bed, on the floor, they were everywhere, yet elegantly so. The bedspread was black satin and on it, was an unopened box of Belgian chocolates, a bottle of red wine and a CD.

'Twinky must have told the family we didn't get to make the baby in Scotland,' I said, still scanning the room.

'Well it isn't right that all this effort goes for waste,' Rish said. 'Why don't you find Twinky's little gift from the suitcase?' he winked.

'I say, we begin with the chocolates and wine and see where they lead us,' I said, jumping on the bed and unwrapping the box.

'I agree,' he said pouncing on me and pecking my chocolate away from my mouth.

'You want to play rough now?' I said tackling him to the bed and spanking his face with the pillow.

'It's what every boy dreams of,' he said, pushing me back onto the bed and grabbing the wine bottle.

'But first, let's shower,' I said and he sighed extra loud.

'Good things come to those who wait,' I said and pulled my nightwear out of the suitcase and headed to the bathroom. It had only been about three seconds before I screamed for Rish to come and take a look. Hanging on the towel hanger was a lacy camisole, and a satin blindfold. On the tub were all kinds of bath and body lotions, scrubs and creamy, moisturizing baths.

'Okay, now it's just getting downright creepy,' Rish said.

'I would have thought this was a touch too far for even Reshu periamma,' I said, 'but to think my mom could have been involved in this!' I winced.

'I must commend their taste though,' he said, running his fingers on the camisole.

'Shut up!' I said and walked back to the room.

'Oh come *on*, I'm a deprived man, show some mercy,' he said, holding out the camisole and putting on his best puppy face.

'Fine,' I said taking the black lace from him, 'make sure the wine is flowing when I'm out.'

He skipped away, delighted.

When I stepped out of the bathroom in the black lace, it felt more than awkward. For starters, the camisole was a size too small, making me look more slutty than sexy and Rish was in his black Calvin Klein boxers as opposed to the usual, checked ones. It was just all wrong – too made-up, too steamy, too unlike *us*.

'Whew,' Rish said eyeing me like it was the first time.

'Really?' I said, genuinely puzzled by his reaction.

'Drink,' he ordered, thrusting a glass of wine in my hand.

'Music,' I ordered back, taking my first gulp.

He obeyed like a good puppy and inserted the CD lying on the bed, into the player.

'I hope it isn't 60s Bollywood,' he said, pecking me on the lips and gulping down his share of wine.

'Or Carnatic hits I said,' kissing him back.

He ran his fingers through my hair and pulled me forward for what would have been a passionate kiss, when we heard Karthick saying something that sounded like corny, high-school mush talk.

'Oh my God,' we both screamed as we realized it was coming from the speakers.

Rish quickly turned the thing off and I sat on the floor against the wall, trying to breathe.

'This whole thing was Karthick's idea,' I said slowly, processing the last half hour. 'Probably for him and Kitty!'

'Do you think they're coming here now?' Rish said and we heard someone sticking a key through the main door.

Too many things followed in the next twenty minutes – Rish and I rushed to the bathroom to change, Karthick walked in with a chick who was not Kitty from any angle and we all screamed different things together.

'What the hell?' I yelled, looking at the pair of them in disgust.

'Could you please ask your lady friend to step out while we talk to you?' Rish asked Karthick in his classic gentleman style.

'Uhh . . . ummm,' Karthick stuttered as we closed the door on the confused girl. 'What are you both doing here?' he said, looking flushed.

'We are living in our apartment, that's what we're doing,' I said, completely losing it.

'But you were supposed to stay at Reshu periamma's place tonight,' he said. 'Didn't they tell you? It's my bachelor party!'

'Well I don't see any bachelors here,' Rish said calmly, *'and we thought it was last night.'*

'Or are they coming too,' I asked, 'dragging their respective cheating partners?'

'I wasn't cheating on Kitty,' Karthick said.

'Really?' I yelled. 'Well I'd love to hear what you were planning on doing with your new chick and all the candles, chocolates and wine, then.'

'And the camisole, blindfold and corny CD,' Rish added with a smile.

'It's not like that!' Karthick pleaded. 'I've just never been with anyone else before and I was nervous about getting married,' he gasped.

'I needed practice,' he added sheepishly.

Suddenly Rish looked like he could forgive him.

'Practice?' I threw my hands up and I could feel my blood pressure shooting up.

'Deeps,' Rish said, trying to calm me down.

'Don't Deeps me,' I snapped.

'Let it go, it's a guy thing,' he said.

'Really?' I asked. 'Did *you* get any "practice" before me?'

'No,' he answered sincerely.

'Well, guess what?' I screamed. 'I could never tell!'

Rish looked like he could kiss me then and there, but I had to turn my attention to Karthick whose head was now hung in shame, embarrassment and school-boyish fear that we would tell the family and Kitty.

'That's the thing about being in love, Karthick,' Rish explained, taking a paternal tone, 'you get to practise on each other,' .

And once again, we had successfully emerged as the super-corny, 'model couple'.

Rish tried to say something to me, after the camisole and blindfold were packed, Karthick sent home and the candles blown out, but I didn't want to hear it.

'Shhh,' I said, putting my finger to his lips, 'you had too much wine.'

'Maybe,' he said, 'wine makes me not want to kill you.'

'True,' I said, 'but I think we need a divorce to ensure it.'

'Tomorrow then?' he asked, 'Dinner and a divorce?'

'Sounds like a plan,' I said.

Twenty-Three

'**S**o, all set to meet the lawyer?' Rish asked me the next morning over coffee.

'We are really doing this,' I said looking up from the newspaper, as the reality of it all hit me.

'We are really doing this,' he confirmed, now that he wasn't under the influence of red wine.

'When are we going to tell them and how are we going to work it all out?' I asked.

'I don't know,' he said, 'we can figure the hows later, but we have to do this now or they will never let us!'

'Yes,' I nodded with sudden resolve.

'Before they hear of last night's incident and anoint us "model couple" all over again,' I said.

'Right,' he agreed, 'we can't let them decide for us again.'

And with that, we proceeded to reclaim our lives back from our families, friends, extended families and random strangers who seemed hell-bent on making our relationship out to be an example of marital bliss.

'So, how long have you both been separated?' Mr Gopalakrishnan our lawyer asked, eyeing the pair of us sceptically. He was a half-bald man in his fifties, who wore a full-sleeved indigo shirt, a tie that didn't match and sat in a plush office that spoke volumes about the number of rich, gullible clients he had milked.

'Umm, actually we've not been separated,' Rish explained, making the man look at us like we were something in a glass case at a museum.

'So, you both woke up on the same bed in the same house this morning, decided to take off from work and go see a lawyer together to discuss your divorce today?'

I decided I didn't like his tone so I refused to answer.

'Well I don't see how that's relevant,' Rish said, letting the annoyance show.

'Well Mr Khanna, it is,' the lawyer said, 'you'll need to be separated for two years to qualify for a divorce by mutual consent.'

He turned to me. 'It's the law,' he said with finality.

'Can't you do something?' Rish resorted to pleading.

'Do what?' the lawyer asked 'Have you both seen a counsellor?'

'No,' Rish said.

'How come your families haven't sent you to a counsellor?' Mr Gopalakrishnan looked upset at our families' negligence.

'Well we haven't exactly told our families yet,' I said and Rish looked at me horrified, like I wasn't supposed to say that.

'What?' the lawyer asked in a tone that sounded like disbelief. 'How could you keep this from your families?'

'Well with all due respect sir,' I said equally shocked at this man's audacity to intrude in our personal matters, 'that is none of your business.'

Rish shot me another what-the-hell-are-you-doing look but I couldn't care. Mr Gopalakrishnan glowered at me the way a schoolmaster does at an insolent student.

'Umm, what she's trying to say is that,' Rish cleared his throat, 'we have about forty thousand rupees set aside for this now,' and the lawyer's face beamed about 500 watts brighter.

'And we've heard good things about you and how you always manage to get things done,' Rish continued, adding, 'somehow'.

I couldn't believe it. I knew for a fact that a divorce by mutual consent didn't cost much more than 20,000 rupees. Rish was blatantly bribing the lawyer!

'I've always encouraged only ethical practices in my firm,' Mr Gopalakrishnan said, making me cringe on behalf of Rish.

'How completely embarrassing,' I thought, when he continued talking.

'However, I see that you are a genuine case,' he said putting on his fake empathetic face, 'so I will see what I can do.'

'Thank you,' Rish said, 'it's really appreciated.'

'This is what I love about India,' I thought, 'there's almost nothing that money can't buy.'

'Well, whatever makes you young people happy,' he said grinning like a saint.

I thanked him for my part and we stood up to leave.

'I will require a 75 per cent advance to proceed with all the work,' our ethical lawyer said, still keeping his obnnoxious grin.

'Oh well, I could write a cheque,' Rish said and proceeded to sign it and hand it over to him.

The greedy man was now beyond delighted and offered us a choice of beverages and when we said no, he insisted that we have tea and samosa with him. He chatted with us merrily about divorce rates and how sad it was that couples were splitting up, but that in genuine cases like ours, there was no other choice and that he hoped we would be happy soon. When we finally got done swallowing our samosas and gulping down our tea, he walked us out to the parking lot himself, waved us goodbye and asked us to come back in a week.

'So, we are 75 per cent divorced,' I said, getting into the car.

'I believe so,' my knight-in-rusty-armour agreed, as we drove away into the sunset.

Twenty-Four

We spent the next couple of days, catching up on sleep. When the Old Wives Club tried to barge into the apartment, they found it locked from the inside and concluded we were making babies. After two days' rest, I looked forward to getting back to work and seeing people who discussed things other than weddings and babies.

I wanted to get my hands on a brief and crack a campaign over several mugs of coffee without any interruption. I wanted to work late nights and do everyone's share of ideation. But most of all, I needed to figure out what I wanted to do for life. I knew advertising wasn't the answer. And foolish as it sounded to me, Rish was as clear as the 9:00 a.m. sky, about his plans of becoming a novelist, but I seemed to resent him more for his clarity, as opposed to his seeming decision to steal my dream.

'What do I really, really, really, really want?' I asked myself as I drove to work that day. Rish had left for a meeting with his colleague and I got our car for the day.

'What are you really, really, really, really good at?' I heard the voice of the failed psychotherapist in my head.

'I don't know,' I answered the voice, 'sometimes I think I can read minds.'

'Well, then do it,' she answered.

'Do what?' I asked out loud. 'Become a psychic?'

'Psychics aren't mind-readers, you fool,' she said.

'What the hell,' I thought, 'I'm talking to an auditory hallucination.'

'I'm not a hallucination!' she screamed.

'Well I'm too old for imaginary friends,' I said, 'so I'd rather you remain a hallucination.'

'I am your inner voice,' she said very solemnly.

'Okay, inner voice,' I said, 'what should I do?'

'I can't tell you that,' she answered.

'I see,' I said. 'Why don't you go annoy someone else then? Like Rish?'

'He has his own inner voice,' she said. 'He calls him the Guru.'

'You mean the one he met in that ashram near Mahabalipuram?' I asked.

'Yes,' she answered, 'and trust me, you don't want him for your inner voice.'

'Why?' I asked, 'Rish seemed to like him!'

'Rish liked him when he asked him to become a writer,' she said. 'But now he's at conflict with the Guru.'

'How the hell do *you* know that?' I asked.

'Do you want to know what he's in conflict about or not?' she got edgy.

'Yes, yes I do,' I said, 'why is he not listening to the Guru?'

'Because the Guru was not supportive of your divorce.'

'I see, so what about you? Do you support it?'

'I don't give yes or no answers. I only lead you to the truth.'

'Very convenient,' I said, 'so what is the truth?'

'You'll know when you get there. In life, there are no short cuts.'

'Stop speaking in riddles and help me at least figure out what I want to do!'

'I already told you, why not read minds?'

'I wish you would tell me what you mean by that,' I screamed aloud.

She laughed and exited as I got the car into the office parking lot.

'Aha! Look who's back,' Swetha waved at me, making the entire office take their eyes off their Facebook pages.

'So, how are the perpetually-horny-not-so-newly-weds doing?' Matthew stepped in.

'Not too bad, actually,' I said and I was surprised at how happy I felt to be back there.

'So, what do you have lined up for me today?' I asked Matthew eagerly, 'I'm sure there's heaps and heaps of work to catch up on?'

'You're actually asking Matthew for work?' Prathiba joined us.

'Yeah babe, it's kind of creepy how happy you are,' Swetha said.

'Leave her alone,' Matthew interrupted, dragging me into the conference room for a briefing.

It was amazing how thankful I felt to have a job and unreasonable clients who wanted 'the ad to go to print at 6 o' clock today'. I grabbed my first mug of coffee and parked myself at my favourite place near the window of the conference room and began poring over briefs, old brochures and other marketing collateral.

'I could spend this whole day and night doing this,' I thought, 'if it meant I didn't have to go home to my family, in-laws and 75 per cent ex-husband.'

'Lunch?' Swetha stood with her hands on her hips before me at 2 p.m. sharp.

'Or do you not have such mortal needs anymore?' Prathiba stared me down.

'Okay, okay I'm coming,' I said, putting my notepad and pen aside.

We landed up at our favourite lunch spot – the food court in Spencer Plaza, where the girls harassed me to give them details of my super-charged sex life.

'If you two remember, Rish and I were planning on getting a divorce,' I said.

'Dude, seriously, who are you kidding?' Prathiba said rolling her eyes.

'It's okay, we're not *that* mad that you're *that* happy,' Swetha said.

'I'm *not* that happy,' I snapped. 'And we are already 75 per cent divorced!' I blurted out.

'What on earth is a 75 per cent divorce?' Prathiba laughed.

'Yeah, it's like being a *little* pregnant,' Swetha added.

'It means we've met a lawyer, initiated proceedings and paid him a 75 per cent advance,' I elucidated.

'You're kidding,' Prathiba said. 'Babe, have you guys seen a counsellor?'

'Stop it,' I threw both hands in the air and got up to leave. I was tired of everyone dispensing unsolicited gyan. Whatever happened to friends who supported you no matter what?

'How are your families taking it?' Swetha called out as I walked out of the food court.

'So much for a great first day at work after vacation,' I thought when I heard the voice again.

'Why does it bother you so much?' she asked.

'Why does what bother me?' I wanted to bite her head off.

'Why do you want everyone to approve of the divorce?' she said.

'I don't want approval,' I said, 'I could settle for acceptance.'

'I'm a lesbian,' she said.

'What?' I screamed. 'What the hell are you saying?'

'See?' she said. 'You're not very accepting either.'

'You're being ridiculous!' I yelled. 'How the hell do I care what the sexual orientation of my hallucination is?'

'Correction, inner voice,' she said. 'And your family and friends will get over it. They have their own crap to sort out and you're not that important.'

'Well, good then. That settles it.'

'Yes. Congratulations on your 75 per cent divorce!'

'Thank you,' I said, gritting my teeth and hoping she'd go away.

I reached home much earlier than I expected that evening and found Rish lying on the couch reading a book titled *What is your inner voice saying?*

'Well played,' I thought, 'very well played.'

The inner voice chuckled.

Twenty-Five

The weekend arrived even before I could tell myself that we didn't have to see the family till the weekend. There was lunch at my parents' place and the entire aunty-uncle cohort was supposed to gather together along with random, hyper-excited cousins to see the wedding trousseau Kitty had got from Delhi.

I had a splitting headache, at the mere thought of what I had to endure the entire afternoon and decided to back out and curled back into bed. But knowing my terrible weakness for a nice-smelling man who asks nicely, Rish came out of the shower smelling like Hugo Man and whispered in my ears to please not abandon him with Reshu periamma. I relented.

Two hours later, when we were neck-deep in pre-nuptial excitement, I cursed Rish. And Hugo Boss for clouding my judgement.

In the living room, our families were seated in an obnoxious way exclusive to our families – boys' side on the left and girls' side on the right. Meaning, he got the giggly, over-excited cousins for company and I got Reshu periamma.

'Oh my god!' the girls howled as Kitty displayed a peacock blue and blood red lehenga bearing the name of one of the country's top-notch designers.

'Very nice ma, very nice,' the aunties from my side approved, while the uncles chose to shake their heads.

'Tell them how much you spent on it!' Dimple aunty urged.

'A lakh and change,' Kitty announced, waiting for everyone to do the traditional eyebrow raise.

Instead, the left side of the room, made a collective 'tch-tch' sound, their prudent-with-finances Tamilian sensibilities hugely offended.

The members of the right side then looked at each other, puzzled by the reaction of the groom's side and my mother-in-law decided to intervene and offer an explanation

'See, we might have done Rish and Deepu's wedding very differently because that is what they wanted,' she said, 'but Kitty wants a full-blown, grand, Punjabi wedding.'

'Deepu and Rish's wedding was grand,' my mother took offence.

'Well, yes, it was a beautiful wedding and everyone loved it,' Dimple aunty tried to pacify my mom, 'but it wasn't the typical, grand, Punjabi wedding na?'

'I think we have a very different idea of what grand is,' my father said and everyone looked amazed that any sound could come out of him.

'What about Karthick?' Rish's dad asked, 'What does *he* want?'

'I just want Kitty,' he answered like a 70s Bollywood hero and everyone went 'awwwwwww'.

'I don't care either,' Kitty sniffed, 'let's have the wedding any way, it doesn't matter.'

Rish and I exchanged eyerolls and Karthick shot us a pleading look that reminded me of scented candles, red wine, lacy camisoles, blindfolds and a hot chick who was *not* Kitty. But I decided to be kind and kept my peace.

'We still have to decide about the wedding,' Mohan uncle said.'The Tamilian way or the Punjabi way?'

'Ours is simple and cost-effective and we can save the money to give the children a nice honeymoon,' my father said.

'Ours is a grand wedding that everyone will talk about,' Rimple aunty said dreamily.

'With flowers flown in from The Netherlands,' Dimple aunty added.

'That is all fine,' Reshu periamma said, 'but we are simple people.'

'They can still go on the honeymoon,' Chandu uncle tried to firm up the argument, but the left side did not look convinced and continued tch-tching.

'It is our tradition to present the children with a reasonably big gift,' Raju uncle said and the tch-tching stopped abruptly. Some of the people from the left side even looked up.

'A Honda City,' Dimple aunty announced and the room fell into respectful silence.

'Well, since you're this insistent, I suppose it's best to do it your way,' Reshu periamma smiled benevolently, conveniently forgetting all about her point on simplicity.

'Yes, I think Reshu's right,' all the ladies on the left side agreed, though my father remained silent.

And before Rish and I could get a chance to exchange eye-rolls again, the wedding crew was playing some Sukhbir-type re-mix number and doing the Balle Balle, making my headache compound to epic proportions.

I waded through lunch, thankful that the spotlight was not on us for a change and sneaked into the guest bedroom later, when Kitty picked up the wedding trousseau display where she left off. Rish, exhausted from evading his father the entire afternoon, decided to step out to the terrace, for a late-afternoon walk.

The weather was cloudy and Rish always thought it was the perfect weather for a quiet walk outside. Only problem was, his father thought so too. So while I curled up obliviously in bed, Rish was having the most awkward confrontation he had had all week. After a good hour and a half of napping, my churning stomach finally woke me up and I joined the wedding crew in the living room.

'Where were you all this time, didi?' Kitty asked as I sat myself down on the divan.

'Was napping inside, Kits,' I said, taking a cup of tea from Reshu periamma's tray.

'Alone?' Suhana asked and all the little ones giggled.

'That reminds me,' I said, 'where the hell is Rish?'

Everyone looked around but no one seemed to know. So I just shrugged and sipped my tea as the cousins made wedding plans and the aunty-uncle cohort gushed about the Honda City.

I don't know what special ingredient Reshu periamma added to the tea that day, but it made my stomach churning so much worse, making me want to throw up.

'Where the hell are you?' I texted Rish, fighting my urge to vomit all over Kitty's lakh-worth lehenga.

Just then, the door opened and Rish and his father appeared together with that 'We just talked it all out' look written on their faces.

'Dear God, please don't tell me he told him already,' I prayed.

'Deepika!' Rish's father pinned me down with his signature penetrating glare, 'We need to talk, beta.'

I threw up.

The good news was that it did not reach Kitty's lehenga. The bad news was that everyone decided I was pregnant. The embarrassing news was that I was not. The scary news was that the aunty cohort wanted to take me to the gynae right away.

Twenty-Six

If Dr Sheena was amused to see three giggly women well into their fifties, drag a grown-up woman into her office to confirm a pregnancy, she did a good job of not letting it show.

'Who's the patient?' Dr Sheena asked all four of us.

'It's me, doctor, Deepika,' I said.

'And what brings you here?' she asked, making it a point to look only at me.

'We tried a home-pregnancy test that came out negative,' my mother-in-law began explaining.

'So, we just wanted to confirm, just to be sure,' my mother smiled.

'And what made you think you were pregnant?' the doctor asked, still looking only at me.

'Actually doctor,' I started, but Reshu periamma interrupted.

'She vomited!' she beamed like I had just brought home an Olympic medal.

'That could just be indigestion,' the doctor said looking bored. 'What else? Did you have a missed period?'

'No, it's not until day after,' I said and the women exchanged anxious glances.

'Come and lie down, Deepika,' Dr Sheena showed me the patient bed behind the curtain, 'I'll need to do a pelvic exam just to be sure.'

'Oh dear,' I thought. I had never been to a gynae before and I was scared to death of pelvic exams. My fear only multiplied by a few thousands as the nurse instructed me to relax, while the doctor got her hand into a glove and poured what seemed like half a bottle of Vaseline on it.

'Relax, Deepika,' Dr Sheena said, looking at my petrified face. 'Nothing you haven't done before.'

I could hear the women giggling behind the curtain and cursed Rish for not being the one with the uterus.

'This is scary, humiliating and utterly pointless,' I thought.

'You have to relax, Deepika,' Dr Sheena said again as the gloved hand drew closer, 'or it will hurt you.'

'Aaaaaaaaaaaaaaaaaaa!' I screamed, but it didn't seem to stop her.

'Have you even had intercourse?' she looked amused as she finished the job.

'It's been a while,' I whispered, so only she could hear, 'but don't tell them!'

Outside, I could tell the women were anxious given the complete silence from their end.

'So how did you think you got pregnant?' Dr Sheena whispered back. 'Hugging? Kissing? Pollination?'

'I didn't think, they did!' I whispered again. Dr Sheena smiled knowingly.

'She is not pregnant,' she announced to the women as I made my way back to my chair.

'But she was vomiting!' my mother-in-law said as if that settled it.

'Yes and you should give her some Gelusil,' Dr Sheena winked at me.

I liked her already. 'If I ever have a baby, I'll come back here,' I made a mental note.

'This doctor seems useless, ma,' my mother decided on our way back.

'Yes, yes,' Reshu periamma joined her. 'She must be a quack!'

'Maybe we should get a second opinion,' my mom-in-law had a bright idea.

'No!' I said firmly and loudly. 'Listen to yourselves! *This* was your second opinion! The home-pregnancy test was the first!'

'Yes ma, but what's the harm in confirming?' my mother continued talking, as if I wasn't screaming and totally losing my cool already.

We got down from the car and made our way through the play area of the apartment complex, to the elevator on the ground floor.

'Listen to me,' I screamed, 'I am *not* pregnant because I *can't* be!'

At this point, some of the neighbours turned around to look at us and all three women hushed me down immediately.

'Are you on the pill?' my mom asked, the minute we stepped into the elevator.

'No!' I snapped. 'God.'

'Oh my God,' Reshu periamma said, making her signature drama-queen face. 'Is it Rish? Does he have problems?'

'There is nothing wrong with my son!' my mom-in-law shot back.

I sighed and rested my head against the elevator wall.

'Are *you* having any problems beta?' my mother-in-law asked me, 'Because I know this really good fertility specialist.'

'What? Nobody in our family has fertility issues!' my mother snapped, as if her only daughter had just been accused of something cringe-worthy like stalking or shoplifting.

'Phew!' I thought, 'Maybe they're just not *meant* to get it.'

When we entered the house, I shot Rish a murderous look for screwing up my day – making me come to lunch, telling his dad about our divorce prematurely and making me barf, and allowing the baby squad to drag me to a gynae and have me poked at, laughed at and utterly humiliated.

'You had no business telling your dad without consulting me,' I breathed into his ears the minute we got some privacy.

'Tell him what?' he asked.

'About our divorce, obviously,' I said. 'You should have seen the look he shot me when you both entered.'

'Are you crazy?' he laughed. 'I didn't tell him anything about the divorce.'

'What?' I couldn't believe it. 'Why was he looking at me like that then?'

'I don't know? We were talking about my writing plans.'

'Oh dear God,' I said. 'You mean I threw up for nothing and endured all of this for absolutely *nothing*?'

'Why, would you rather I told him now?'

'No! But how did the talk go?'

'Began with disbelief, gradually moved to anger, denial and indifference and I think we finally managed to hit acceptance.'

'Good for you,' I said. 'But just so you know, your mom thinks I'm barren and mine thinks you're impotent.'

He laughed, 'I'll remember to mention that to the lawyer.'

Twenty-Seven

'**W**elcome! Welcome!' Mr Gopalakrishnan was extra chirpy as we walked into GKB Legal on Monday.

'Sounds like a Chettiar-run jewellery shop,' I whispered to Rish, looking at the name board.

'Good evening Mr Gopalakrishnan,' Rish said politely as he shook his hand and sat down.

'Tea? Coffee?' the pot-bellied man made the usual polite enquiries.

'No, thank you,' we both said.

'Horlicks? Bournvita? Badam milk?' he continued.

'No really, we're fine,' I said. 'Thank you.'

'Samosa? Egg puffs? Bajji?'

'We'll have coffee,' Rish relented finally and Mr Gopalakrishnan looked pleased.

'So, tell me,' he said, rubbing his palms together gleefully.

'Uhh . . . you had asked us to come on Monday,' Rish reminded him.

'Right, yes, I wanted to ask you both some questions before drafting your petition.'

'Ask away,' I said.

'Have you both discussed all property matters?'

'What property?' Rish asked.

'Basically, who gets what.'

'We really don't have much,' I said.

'Nothing at all?' Mr Gopalakrishnan asked again, 'TV? Music system? Fridge? Any high-end furniture? A pet? Nothing?'

'Uhh,' Rish said, 'well . . .'

I blinked.

'You both really have no idea how this is done, do you?'

'Do all the other couples who come here, know?' I asked.

'Well for starters, they don't come to me together because they are usually separated and when they see each other, they fight!' he smiled smugly. 'You both never fight!'

'Well, we will be separated too,' Rish said. 'We're just waiting for a wedding in the family after which we will break the news and get separated.'

'And we do fight!' I said, trying hard to remember our last fight.

'So why can't you wait till after the wedding?' Mr Gopalakrishnan probed.

'Do you want to return my advance?' Rish lost it.

'Relax, Mr Khanna, please relax,' he attempted to pacify him.

'Shankar! Oru glass water konduva!' he ordered the office boy.

'We would just like to get this over with as soon as possible,' I said.

'Yes, I understand madam,' he said, 'I just need to be sure you both definitely want to be divorced.'

'I paid you a 75 per cent advance on a fee that's clearly double the regular mutual-consent fee!' Rish's BP shot up. 'Why would I do that if we were not sure?'

'Fine then, Mr Khanna!' the gleeful face was back on. 'Just send me a mail stating who is keeping what and I'll draft the petition at the earliest!'

'Thank you,' we both said as we got up to go.

Rish was silent as we drove back.

'We do fight,' I said.

He smiled shortly.

'I mean, I think your family is completely obnoxious,' I said. 'You should have heard your mom calling me barren, yesterday. It was the limit!'

He nodded silently.

'I'm keeping the TV, the music system and the Playstation!'

'Anything to get you interested in the Playstation,' he smiled.

'Why are you being so eerily nice?'

'Why are you trying so hard to pick a fight?'

'Because that's *us*. We fight.'

'I can't remember our last one.'

'Me neither, but it was all your fault.'

'Well, I'm sorry,' he said smiling and his eyes welled up.

It was my turn to keep silent.

I tossed and turned all night, too afraid to broach the topic with Rish, yet too restless to be left in the dark. What was he thinking? Did he not want to be divorced anymore? Or was he just shedding sentimental tears for old times' sake? Was he too chicken to let the family know? The questions wouldn't stop. Then the failed psychotherapist showed up in my mind's eye again to make my night doubly exhausting.

'What do *you* want?' she started.

'I want a divorce, obviously!'

'Would that change if Rish didn't want it?'

'Maybe?'

'Aha! Then you're not sure!'

'Maybe I'm not, what's your point?' I was sleep-deprived and irritated.

'My point is you might want to stop that lawyer.'

'Why can't *he* stop him?'

'Why are you talking like you're twelve?'

'So, what are you saying now, that I should stop the divorce?'

'I'm not saying anything! I'm your inner voice, I can only help you find your answers, not hand them to you on a platter.'

'Fine then,' I said,'I'm getting the divorce.'

'Fine.'

Over the next few days, Rish and I managed to successfully avoid each other by spending late nights at work, but the weekend came pounding on our door sooner than we'd expected.

'We have to prepare the family for the divorce,' Rish said as we got ready to head to my parents' house again.

'And how do we do that?' I asked brushing my hair.

'By not coming across as the model couple,' he said.

'And how do we do *that*?' I smiled.

'I have no idea,' he said.

'Rish?' I asked in a few minutes. 'Are you having any doubts about this?'

'No,' he said. 'You?'

'No.'

'See? He'll never admit it!' I said to my inner voice as we got into the car.

'Maybe he doesn't know how to,' she said. 'Why don't you show him?'

I shot a glance at Rish, driving as if everything was fine with the world.

'Huh. Fat hopes,' I said.

'You two deserve each other,' she sighed.

'Look, we had very good reasons for wanting this,' I said, 'I don't see why we should doubt it now!'

'Because your families won't be all right with it?'

'Precisely, we can't let them win!'

'True, that's a very valid reason to get divorced,' she said.

'Oh just go away,' I said and flipped her off like she were a gnat inside my head.

Twenty-Eight

When we entered my parents' house, the scene was pretty much the same as the last gathering, except the bride and groom's side were both seated together. All the girls sat in a circle and animatedly discussed their outfits for the wedding, while the uncle-aunty gang discussed the flowers that were to be flown in from The Netherlands, the white horses that had to be hired to stand at the entrance and take the groom on a grand tour of the hotel lawn and other such everyday wedding props.

I stood against the wall in the corner of the room, watching everyone and avoiding the nuptial excitement as if it were a deadly virus. My mind wandered to Rish, my inner voice and back to Rish several times, making me feel like a fish out of water.

'Maybe I should talk to him,' I thought. 'Maybe we are doing this because we don't want to let them win. Maybe this isn't about us anymore.'

'Deepu, beta!' my mother-in-law came charging in my direction at the first opportunity. 'I need to talk to you.'

'Uhh, hold on aunty, I'll get Rish,' I said.

'Oh I was hoping we could just talk,' she said, 'you know? Woman to woman?'

I raised my eyebrows. 'Uhh, sure, why not?'

'See, I'm sorry if I offended you the other day, it's just that . . .'

'Oh, no offence taken aunty, not to worry.'

'Well, great then, we'll see Dr Rakhi,' she said. 'You can just come with me to Delhi next week. I'll take you, we won't even need Rish around.'

'Sorry? What?' I was confused, 'Who's Dr Rakhi?'

'The fertility specialist of course!'

'Aunty there is nothing wrong with me!' I said.

'Arre, what's the harm in checking beta?'

I looked at Rish from across the room, peacefully indulging in a bowl full of rasgullas all by himself.

'Actually, it's Rish, aunty,' I said, 'I just didn't want to be the one to tell you.'

And with that, I had successfully wriggled out of the baby harassment for the entire afternoon.

'Bitch!' Rish and my inner voice said together.

'Sorry, but what was I to do?' I said.

'You realize you just sentenced me to the most embarrassing conversation of my life with my mom?' Rish said.

'You realize now, what it's like to be the one with the uterus?' I said.

'I am not going to a fertility specialist and jerking off into a cup!'

'Well I went to a gynae and peed on a stick, you know? It's only fair.'

'I cannot believe you!' he said.

'I cannot believe your mom!' I whispered.

'Okay, everyone!' Reshu periamma stood up, clapping her hands to get everyone's attention.

'The wedding is only a couple of weeks away and we need to book tickets to Delhi as soon as possible,' she announced.

'Everyone's going to be there a week in advance, na?' Suhana enquired.

'What? That's not possible!' I said, 'There's no way I'll be able to take off from work again this early.'

'Arre, big deal, beta,' one of the aunties said. 'Just quit then!'

'Correct,' my mother-in-law laughed, 'why do you even need that job? My son didn't go to IIT for nothing. He makes enough money for the both of you!'

'Huh?' is all I could say.

'Yes Deepu, you don't need to work,' another one of the women said absent-mindedly, while flipping a bridal magazine.

'No, no, girls should be independent and stand on their own feet,' my mother said.

'I didn't educate her for nothing,' my father added.

'But she only did M.A. Literature, no? What can you do with that?' Reshu periamma said matter-of-factly.

'You can become a writer with that and that's what she wants to become!' Rish spoke up all of a sudden and the whole room fell silent.

I looked at Rish for a while and in a flash, I knew it.

'I don't want to be a writer,' I said, 'I want to be a psychotherapist.'

'What?' a lot of people said together. Some laughed. Rish looked thoroughly befuddled.

'Yes,' I said. 'That's what I want to be.'

'You want to study all over again?' Suhana asked as if it was the worst thing a person could do with their adulthood.

'I believe so,' I said and looked at Rish, waiting for him to make his announcement. He opened his mouth, when my mother interrupted.

'But that is better than becoming a writer ma,' she said. 'Those people never have money, drink a lot and eventually become mad,' she laughed.

Rish closed his mouth again. His father coughed uncomfortably. And everyone wondered aloud about how the wedding discussion got steered to career counselling.

'You have to tell them at some point,' I said pulling him aside, 'and this seemed like the oportune moment.'

'I just think it will be better if they hear it together with the divorce. One shot, quick and painful.'

'True,' I agreed, 'true.'

That night, a reminder from Mr Gopalakrishnan had landed in our respective inboxes, requesting us to send him the details of our marriage, separation and property. We both stared at it together for a long time, after which Rish got out his bottle of Absolut Raspberry and began typing out the mail. The mail indicated that I could continue staying in our rented apartment and keep everything in it.

'No,' I protested, 'I don't want anything.'

'Neither do I,' he said. 'You can give it to charity if you'd like.'

'Where are you moving?' I asked.

'Far away from the family, the (ex) in-laws, the family friends, neighbours and random relatives.'

'You're leaving the country?'

'Possibly,' he said. 'Not headed anywhere near London though.'

I smiled. 'So, what are we doing about this wedding?'

'Go and bless the couple and hope they don't end up like us?' he smiled back.

I nodded, sipping my drink.

'So, psychotherapist,' he said when we were one glass down, 'what's your expert analysis of our situation?'

'I could tell you, but it won't come cheap.'

'Can I pay in kind?' he winked, 'I'm a soon-to-be penniless writer.'

'You are flirting with your 75 per cent ex-wife!' I said. 'How pathetic is that?'

'Very. Now, can I pay?'

'I haven't even given you the analysis!'

'We can skip that part,' he laughed.

But somehow good sense prevailed and we decided to hit the sack. In separate rooms.

Twenty-Nine

The next few days went away in a blur of family-wedding-fun that I had no choice but to be a part of. For starters, Twinky and Prince decided that showing up unannounced at our apartment and screaming 'surprise' would somehow make us very happy. So we decided it was our turn to return the hospitality and welcomed them home after they had told everyone, they were staying at our place anyway.

My time at office was no better, with Swetha and Prathiba constantly asking questions and even giving me the occasional cold shoulder, Mayura apologizing for 'being such a jerk' previously and Matthew asking me if I wanted to talk every time I sat by the window to crack an ad. Almost my entire circle at work had heard about our divorce plans and from the thickness in the air that hung over us, I could tell that not one of them approved of it.

'It's funny,' I thought, 'in the movies, they make it look like the hardest thing for lovers is to convince the Indian family about their decision to marry each other, but try getting divorced and the whole society protests!'

'You know, I can help,' Mayura came up to me during lunch hour, 'Nitin and I once came very close to a divorce.'

'But you didn't get divorced,' I said.

'Exactly.'

'Why didn't you?'

'Well,' she started.

'You know what, just save it,' I snapped. 'You gave in to your family's wishes and that's not a very inspiring story for me right now.'

'Well I did, but only because I realized they were right.'

'Really? So you and Nitin don't fight anymore?'

'We do, but it's usually about the toilet seat!' she laughed.

'Well, Rish and I have bigger differences,' I said and walked out.

I was actually happy to leave work early that day, though it meant having dinner with the family at Mainland China. The wedding was only a week away and pre-nuptial euphoria was at an all-time peak. We had taken a massive space in the restaurant and thanks to the Punjabi side of the family, everyone in the restaurant soon heard everything that was going on in our family – Kitty and Karthick's wedding, Arvind's mothballs (which was now a joke in the family), our Two States wedding, everything. What's more, Twinky had brought her share of our UK holiday stories that everyone in the family quickly lapped up.

'You have a BMW 7 series?' Karthick's eyes popped out as Twinky consciously peppered the conversation with details of her life as The Princess.

Rimple aunty beamed with pride as her firstborn droned on about the complexities of being married to the son of a renowned business tycoon.

'Oh and that's the car Rish bhaiya and Deepu didi traded for the train to Edinburgh,' she said.

'What?' Karthick looked horrified at the sacrilege we had committed.

'But the train was fun too,' Twinky obliged. 'How is your writing coming along bhaiya?'

Rish and I tried very hard to signal to her to shut up, but Twinky wasn't looking at us.

'What writing?' someone from the table asked and Twinky proceeded to give a detailed report of Rish's plans to switch careers.

A collective 'What' swept through the dinner table and Rish started humming *The Godfather* tune.

Luckily, the waiter had come over to take our orders and that kept the family busy for the next twenty minutes. First, the Punjabi side ordered every possible chicken preparation on the menu, along with soups, salads, vegetables and anything that sounded fancy.

After that, the Tamilian side simply asked the waiter to make everything 'One by two'. Rish's side exchanged looks with each other utterly nonplussed, while my side of the family couldn't stop calculating costs, asking repeatedly 'but why so many items?'

Thankfully, by the time we got done with our orders, everyone had forgotten about Rish's career switch and the topic had returned to the wedding and us being the model couple.

'This wedding is going to be the talk of the town,' my mother-in-law said, 'Dimple just called from Delhi.'

And that's when I realized that the bride and her parents were not even present at the dinner table. With the number of family members we had to deal with in the recent past, it was hard enough remembering who was related to whom and which aunties were Rish's and which ones were mine, given that they seemed to blend so seamlessly these days with all the drain-pipe jeans and Cha-Cha*ing*.

'I cannot wait,' Suhana clapped her hands together in wide-eyed joy, like a five-year-old who was going to be taken to the beach.

'It's going to be in Oberoi,' my mother-in-law sounded pleased.

'It's not our style but as long as everybody's happy,' Reshu periamma said, picking at her tooth.

'Oh I'm sooo happy,' Twinky said making her signature shriek and turning heads in our direction.

We were the last to clear the table and I could tell the staff couldn't wait for us to leave.

It was 11:40 in the night when we got back to our apartment with Twinky and Prince. I was exhausted, mentally and physically and the thought of waking up to another day at work, only made me want to hit the sack right away. But Twinky like most other women in the family seemed to think that work was what mortals did to afford their butter chicken and certainly was not for anyone married to anyone in her bloodline.

Rish and Prince chatted in the balcony sipping their beers with Prince doing all the talking and Rish nodding and yawning at alternate intervals.

'I'm going to take a pregnancy test now!' Twinky whispered to me excitedly at ten minutes past midnight.

'You think you're pregnant?' I asked stupidly.

'I think so, but I haven't said anything to anyone yet,' she said, 'not even Raja!'

'Wow,' I thought, 'the woman can actually keep a secret.'

'My period was supposed to come day before yesterday,' she said, 'and there's still no sign of it.'

'Aah,' I said, 'well, take your test then.'

'You have to come with me and read it for me!'

'Uhh. Okay.'

Twinky came out of the bathroom after doing her business and picked out four names in the three minutes that I had to wait with her for the result.

'Tarun, I'll call him Tarun,' she beamed at me as if she was in the maternity ward and I was the old midwife who announced, 'It's a boy!'

'Twinky, let's wait,' I said. I shuddered to imagine the tantrum that would surely follow if the test results turned out negative.

'You're right didi, what if I'm not pregnant? We've been trying for two months now! I'll never live it down!'

A tear trickled down her cheeks and I began to wonder if it was an indication of pregnancy hormones.

'What if it's a girl?' I tried to undo the damage.

'Rihanna,' she beamed once again as if she hadn't had palpitations just a few seconds ago.

'You mean after the singer?'

'Yes. Isn't she brilliant?'

'Uhh, sure. Of course.'

'Or Robin,' she said as if it was just another traditional Punjabi name.

'Robin?'

'Yeah, Robin Scherbatsky from *How I Met Your Mother*! Don't you watch the show? I love her!'

'Right. Of course. I'm sure everyone will love it!'

'Oh actually, Aryan if it's a boy, not Tarun.'

'I love that name,' I said surprised that we had similar taste in something.

'At home, we will call him Bunty of course,' she clarified.

'And it's time!' I made my way inside the bathroom hoping with every breath that it was a positive, while Twinky drummed her fingers on the bathroom door, loud enough to give me a headache.

'You've got a pink line!' I called out, 'Congrats!'

'I have a girl?' Twinky shed tears of joy thinking of Robin.

'Uhh no Twinky,' I said, 'they haven't yet found ways to detect the sex of the baby with three drops of urine.'

'But I'm pregnant!' she hugged me.

'That you are!' I hugged her back.

Outside, Prince stood laughing and chatting, with no idea whatsoever about the arrival of Robin or Bunty in his life.

Thirty

Twinky and Prince were still asleep when we left for work the next day. My day disappeared in a string of deadlines that kept me away from lunch, phone calls and harassing conversations with highly intrusive colleagues. I could see people shoot judgemental looks at me every once in a while, but I didn't care. All that mattered was that our shampoo client had packaged his product differently, added jojoba to the ingredients and was making a loud comeback in a week.

There was no time to drown in petty matters such as divorce and judgemental friends. Everyone had to work together as a team to ensure that innocent, undiscerning customers flock to said old shampoo in a new bottle, because of our creative brilliance. And if we had to endure a 'We can do it' pep talk from the creative director for forty precious minutes on account of this, so be it.

Conning the audience was the aim and the client was the unsuspecting fat cow about to be milked like nobody's business. So, come hell, high-waters, weekends or lunch time – ours was not to reason why; ours was but to write clever headlines and lie. This was advertising emergency at its best – flying tempers, narrow deadlines, missed lunches, whiny colleagues, painful client and colourful profanities in the air. Sure, we can't give our lives for the country, perform open-heart surgery or help prevent global warming. But we know how to make people buy things they don't want to buy. And that makes us way cooler than everyone else and gives us the right to walk into office in jeans on weekdays, smoke pot, check our Facebook page before we open our office mail and address even the senior-most people at work as 'Dei Peter!'

'Got a minute?' Prathiba asked me at around ten in the night.

'Sure,' I said, 'what's up?'

'So, what really went wrong with Rish?'

'Are you kidding me?' I said. 'I am trying to crack a whole bunch of concepts here for the jojoba emergency, in case you didn't notice!'

'Trust me, the launch will happen even without your brilliance. Now, tell me what happened.'

'I do not have time for this, Prathiba!' I said, getting up from my chair.

'Deeps!' Matthew called. 'Rish is here for you.'

'What?' I rushed to the reception. What the hell was Rish doing here?

Rish was tapping his feet and waiting at the reception with his palms folded into each other as if waiting at a maternity ward.

'Rish?' I said, 'Is everything all right?'

'Can I just wait here till you finish?'

'Yeah, sure,' I said, 'what happened?'

'Nothing. Just don't want to go home and deal with Twinky and Prince.'

'I think they're staying at my parents' place tonight.'

'Look, I just don't want to be alone tonight, okay?' he said.

'Okay, do you want to get out for a bit?'

'No, just leave me alone!'

'Err. Okay.' I sat by his side.

He was silent for the next fifteen minutes and passers-by shot us curious glances. I decided to order dinner and placed my order for curd rice with the office boy, when Matthew stepped out to tell me I could go.

'But I'm not done yet,' I said.

'Well we can take it from here,' he insisted.

'I don't want to dump my work on someone else's plate,' I said.

'Deeps, just go home,' he said almost imploringly and walked back into the office.

I stared in that direction for two minutes and picked up my bags to leave. Rish remained silent even in the car. We stopped at Gallopin' Gooseberry for a quick bite and he nibbled at his food.

I ordered my favourite lasagne though and attacked it like a pregnant cow gone mad.

'They won't let me go at work,' he finally said.

'What do you mean?' I asked through a mouthful.

'They won't accept my resignation.'

'That's not such a bad thing!' I said, 'Isn't there a way you can keep your job and do your writing?'

'They can't transfer me anywhere else.'

'Oh.'

'I can leave anyway, but I don't want to leave on a bad note. I don't know how this writing thing is going to go.'

'You can have the apartment,' I offered.

'You really think that's my problem?' he snapped, 'Forget it.'

'I would know if you told me!' I said.

'I'm going to the ashram tomorrow,' he said.

'To speak to the Guru?'

He nodded.

'So you can't tell me, but you'll tell the Guru?'

'We're 75 per cent divorced. I might as well get used to it.'

'What are you saying now, Rish? Do you not want to get divorced? Just say it!'

'I'm not saying anything,' he said, sounding annoyingly similar to my inner voice and that was that.

We went home and hit the sack right away. We were both going to have a really long day – he had to leave early in the morning to consult with his Guru in Mahabalipuram and I had an emergency shampoo situation at work.

Thirty-One

I reached work by 9:00 the next morning, a record that hasn't been broken by a copywriter ever since, in the history of Bennet & Cole. We usually strolled in at 11 a.m., checked Facebook, took coffee breaks, gossiped and played table tennis till lunch time, after which we headed to Spencer Plaza and got back around 3:00. At 4:00, we checked out for another coffee and smoke break and checked our work mails around 4:30. We then wasted time till 5:00, asking useless questions and harassing our client servicing people and started work around 6 p.m We still hoped to wind up by 10 p.m. though and managed to leave by 11:00 on most days.

It was only in the case of pitches and emergency situations such as this one, that we informed our families we would see them sometime in the near future and came prepared with our pyjamas to camp at work. We always stepped up then and stayed awake even for thirty hours at a stretch if the situation called for it.

'And what are you doing here so early?' Matthew strolled in yawning at 9:30.

'I'm making up for lost time,' I smiled.

'Oh we didn't miss you,' he said. 'You should be home, working out your marriage.'

'I'm getting marital advice from you!' I said, 'It's almost creepy!'

Matthew was the commitment-phobic stereotype and was known to change girlfriends faster than his socks.

'Exactly. Almost as creepy as you and Rish getting divorced,' he shot back.

'God! Enough about Rish and me already!' I said, 'If you should know, he's currently with his therapist working out his career switch, as opposed to his failing marriage.'

'Rish has got a therapist? Wow.'

'You have no idea,' I thought.

'And what career switch?' he asked.

'Well, he's planning to become a novelist. The full-fledged, stay-at-home variety.'

'Hot. I think *I'm* falling in love with him.'

I ignored him and turned back to my computer.

Prathiba and Swetha strolled in together at 10:45, when I was halfway through my brief.

'Hey! What happened with Rish last night?' Prathiba enquired.

'Nothing,' I said. 'Nothing at all.'

'Rish has a therapist and he's planning to quit his top-notch corporate career to become a novelist,' Matthew announced. 'Now, which one of you wants to grab him when Deepika leaves?'

'Oh go away Matthew,' Swetha swished her hand at him and Prathiba raised hers saying, 'Me! Me!'

I ignored the lot and continued cracking away at my shampoo launch brief. Our afternoon discussion in the conference room was nothing short of a nightmare for me. This was when we sat together with the senior-most people – the account heads, creative director and senior art directors, apart from the annoying client servicing idiots whom we had a love-hate relationship with, and fellow 'creative' people and discussed our ideas – which simply meant that if our ideas sucked, almost the entire office got to watch us making asses of ourselves. And it was my turn that day.

Eight lousy ideas presented one after the other in the ascending order of lousiness, I kept the conference room snickering, snorting and plain guffawing, till Ravi our creative director, gestured to me to stop and asked one of the interns to take over.

'I finally have something worthwhile to fill in that Most Embarrassing Moment slot on scrap books,' I thought.

It was humiliating and made me hide in the bathroom for the next twenty minutes and pray for the day to end.

'I don't just hate what I do, I suck at it,' I thought. 'This isn't me.'

I shuddered at the thought of spending another couple of years in the ad world before saving enough money to support myself while I studied. I was jealous of Rish – that he knew what he wanted, had the talent, the passion and the courage to go after it and the bank balance to support it. He was living the life. But he wasn't happy and I couldn't tell why. I wondered if it was the divorce, but decided not to flatter myself.

'Hey babe,' Swetha said as I got back to my cubicle.

'Chill, it happens. We all have bad days,' she tried to comfort me.

I smiled. I was having a bad year – with work, with Rish, with my future plans.

'I think I'll just head home early today,' I said.

All I wanted was some me-time, soaking in my Iris and Lavender shower cream, with a book in hand. The fact that half the wedding crew was on its way to Delhi, Twinky and Prince were at my parents' place and Rish was with his Guruji, only made the idea all the more inviting.

About half an hour into my blissful nap in the bathtub, I was rudely awoken by the jarring sound of the doorbell. I ignored it the first two times, but it rang again. And again. And again. Till I stepped out, got dressed and answered the door.

'How the hell did Rish get back this early,' I wondered, but it was the baby squad – Twinky, Prince, Rimple aunty, my mother and mother-in-law.

'What is going on with you two?' they charged inside. 'Why aren't you both picking up our calls?'

'It's been a crazy few days at work, 'I said, 'and Rish is away at . . .'

'Bangalore, we know,' his mother said. 'He mentioned he had to be there for an important meeting.'

I nodded, my mouth zipped. 'He should at least keep me posted when he's lying to them,' I thought.

'Didi!' Twinky cut in, 'I'm headed to the gynae now!' she beamed as if she was going on a week-long trip to Bali.

'Uhh, that's great,' I said. 'Now you'll know for sure.'

'Arre, she already knows, beta,' Rimple aunty said. 'She's even taking folic acid.'

'I did some googling,' Twinky announced proudly, 'I'm just going to the gynae to check if it's safe to travel now.'

'Anyway, that doctor is a quack ma,' my mother added.

'Hmmm,' I said, too lazy to argue and decided to hide in the kitchen under the pretence of making tea.

'I know this is a difficult time for you, Deepu beta,' my mother-in-law followed me into the kitchen.

'Sorry, what aunty?' I said.

'You are not pregnant and now Twinky is. It can be hard.'

'What? That's absurd aunty. I'm so happy for Twinky.'

'This is why I insisted on taking you both to Dr Rakhi, but Rish got so mad at me for that,' she continued as if I hadn't spoken a word. I realized there was no winning with my mother-in-law and decided to keep silent.

'Even now it's not too late,' she continued as I directed all my concentration on the water boiling in the kettle.

'We can go when you're in Delhi for the wedding.'

I added tea and sugar without saying a word.

'She's a very busy lady, but I can fix an appointment for you right away. Just say yes!'

I turned around to face her.

'I have no say in this, aunty. You'll have to discuss this with your son.'

She tch-tched and walked away into the living room.

We were about to be divorced within a week and our families were in blissful denial. Actually, it wasn't denial. They had no idea. I wondered if it was reverse psychology. They were so tiresome and obnoxious, they made Rish and I want to stick with each other all the time. We hated having to deal with them alone. I wondered about the awkwardness that would follow with the family once we were officially divorced.

We would invariably bump into each other given that Karthick and Kitty would be married by then. Also, our families were in love with each other, to the point of doing irrational things like Cha-Cha classes and drunken kitty parties. I wondered if all that would continue if Rish and I fell apart publicly. I pictured our families fighting, like the ones in the soaps my mother watched. And I felt a sharp twinge of guilt at the thought of being responsible for their love affair coming to an end. Rish and I would be friends even after the divorce, I knew that for sure. In fact, we would be the best of friends, given that it would be a relationship sans marital expectations. But things would not be the same with our families, I could tell.

And suddenly, I felt like the villainous parent of star-crossed lovers out of an 80s Tamil flick.

Thirty-Two

Forty-five minutes later, we found ourselves in Dr Sheena's office again. This time I was dragged along so that the nice doctor could advise me to see a fertility specialist. The people in the waiting room stared and made faces as we all marched into the doctor's office together – Rimple aunty, Twinky, Prince, my mother, mother-in-law and me.

'Only three people at a time madam,' the nurse said and I felt like hugging her.

'Arre, we just want to invite the doctor to a function, we won't be long,' my mother-in-law lied casually, dragging us all inside.

Dr Sheena looked up at us and I couldn't tell if she was irritated or amused.

'So, you vomited again?' she asked, looking at me.

'Oh she is the one, doctor,' Rimple aunty presented Twinky. 'She's pregnant.'

'And?' Dr Sheena asked Twinky, eyeing everyone else sceptically.

Rimple aunty, Twinky and my mother-in-law took the three chairs on the patient's side, while my mom, Prince and I stood waiting.

'And I'm going back to London by the end of the month,' she said. 'So I'll have to see a doctor there,' she rambled.

'Because that's where they live,' Rimple aunty added proudly, 'she's my daughter.'

'Let me put it this way,' Dr Sheena said as if talking to a three-year-old, 'why are you here?'

'Oh,' Twinky said and the women laughed. 'We just wanted to check if it was okay for me to travel in my condition.'

'What condition?' Dr Sheena asked.

'Well, I'm pregnant!'

'How many weeks?'

'Uhh, I don't know, I took a home-pregnancy test the other day,' Twinky looked at me for support.

'The test was positive, doctor,' I said, doing my bit. Twinky smiled at me.

'Well, I'll have to do a pelvic exam and an ultrasound to confirm. Home-pregnancy tests can go wrong.'

'See? I told you no? She's a quack!' my mother whispered to me.

I gritted my teeth.

Dr Sheena did the pelvic exam and said that it did feel like a pregnancy, but only an ultrasound could confirm that. The women complained that it was completely unnecessary and just the hospital's way of making money. Dr Sheena refused to let anyone other than Twinky and Prince into the ultrasound room and the women took the opportunity to pounce on me.

'You and Rish have nothing to be ashamed of,' Rimple aunty comforted me.

'Thank you aunty, I think we know that,' I said matter-of-factly.

'Then you must see a fertility specialist beta,' she said nudging my mother. 'Tell her!'

'She said Rish was having problems,' my mother answered looking at the floor.

'What? Our Rish? Impossible!' Rimple aunty laughed, 'The men in our family!' and the two sisters blushed and laughed some more.

I could tell my mother was positively annoyed.

Just then, the ultrasound room door opened and Dr Sheena stepped out with a beaming Twinky and a proud albeit mildly nervous Prince. We followed the doctor back into her office, where she confirmed that Twinky was indeed nine weeks pregnant.

'We'd like to know if it's a boy or a girl,' Twinky said.

'It's too early to tell the sex of the baby,' Dr Sheena answered without looking up. 'Besides, it's unlawful for us to reveal it.'

'What?' Twinky asked, 'How are we supposed to know what colour to paint the nursery then?'

Dr Sheena kept writing out a prescription in silence.

'In London, they reveal the sex of the baby all the time!' Twinky continued.

'Then, you should wait till you get to London,' Dr Sheena said, being careful not to smile.

'And we need you to advise her, doctor,' my mother-in-law said, pushing me forward.

'On what?' Dr Sheena asked looking at me quizzically, 'Deepika right?'

I nodded.

'They are having problems conceiving and she is almost thirty. Please advise her on seeing a fertility specialist,' my mother-in-law continued.

'There is nothing wrong with her,' Dr Sheena said firmly. 'Maybe you should all leave her alone with her husband more often,' she said.

'Certified Quack,' my mother whispered to me.

I just cursed Rish under my breath for abandoning me with the baby squad again.

Thirty-Three

It was past midnight when Rish came home and for some reason, I couldn't wait to hear what happened with the Guru. I always suspected Rish confided more to the Guru than he ever did to me and though I had resented the Guru for taking my place in his life earlier, this time, I was just curious – I wanted to know if it was worth the effort of going all the way – Did he get the answer he was looking for? Was he going to stick with Accenture or was he leaving right away? Did he discuss our divorce? What did the Guru have to say about it? I had questions and I couldn't hope to have them answered with the Old Wives Club + Deliriously Happy Pregnant Couple hogging our space and insisting on chatting loudly in our living room.

I ran to the door when I heard Rish coming, so I could warn him about the family taking over the living room and ask him to stick to his Bangalore story. When the door opened and Rish stepped in however, I thought I was the one who could have used a warning – not only did he look eerily calm and placid, he even spoke in an affected, spooky fashion.

'What happened to you?' I asked as he smiled at me patronizingly.

Silence. He walked into the living room and continued smiling at everyone.

'Rish! Thank God you're here,' Prince called out, 'I've been all alone with the ladies for two days! Come on, let me fix you a drink!'

'Nothing for me, thank you,' Rish put on a wispy, chiffon voice.

I stood behind him cautiously, expecting him to faint or just evaporate into thin air any minute.

'Maybe the journey tired him out,' I thought. 'That's probably why he's acting odd and out of sorts.'

'I'm going back to join him,' Rish finally announced looking at me.

'Going where?' his mother asked.

'Uhh, to Bangalore aunty, to join his boss,' I covered up.

Rish was oblivious. 'Yes, that is what gives me peace,' he said, still smiling in the same creepy fashion.

Everyone looked at each other and shrugged.

'Why do you want to go to Bangalore Rish?' my mother asked.

Rish continued smiling.

'I'd like to talk to him,' I said. 'Your boss.'

'You can't talk to him,' Rish answered. 'You have to go and see him,' and he smiled once again in that eerie fashion.

'Fine then,' I said, 'I will leave tomorrow!'

'I sense resentment and bitterness in your tone,' he said, still keeping the smile.

'Damn it, Guru,' I thought. 'What the hell did you do to him?'

'Accha, whatever is going on between you two,' my mother-in-law stepped in, 'solve it! Because I'm taking you both to Dr Rakhi when you're in Delhi. No arguments.'

'What?' I snapped and looked at Rish.

'What we need now is an exorcist, not a fertility specialist!' I muttered under my breath.

He smiled. 'Anything to put a smile on your face ma.'

I never felt more alone. Now I had to deal with two mental families *and* a brainwashed, peace, love and joy spewing nutcase of a husband. I couldn't wait to head to the ashram and give that Guru a piece of my mind. I was always suspicious of god-men. But since this one did not take any money, I hadn't bothered too much. Now I was convinced that this was a major ruse to get Rish working for him.

'So much for IIT,' I said, after we had sent the family away, 'Rishab Khanna, sidekick to Guruji.'

Rish smiled peacefully. 'You won't understand,' he said. 'There is too much negativity in the air.'

I wanted to smash his face with the lamp-stand but decided to get some sleep instead. I had a long, difficult day ahead of me – I had to speak to Ravi our creative director and beg him for another day off, go to the ashram near Mahabalipuram, ask the Guru to fix Rish somehow and get back the following day to make it to the family court for divorce, pack and leave for the wedding.

'Rish,' I said as my last, feeble attempt, 'are you sure you're okay?'

'I've found my peace.'

'Good night,' I said, switching off the bedside lamp.

'Rest your mind,' he said and I wished he would just snore for old times' sake.

'September 7th!' I screamed as I got out of bed and my eyes fell on the calendar, 'Today is September 7th!'

'Right, it's the day we're getting divorced,' Rish said calmly and I noticed the smile was still on.

'I've been thinking the divorce is day after!' I was having an anxiety attack. How on earth would I be able to explain this to Ravi, given that the shampoo emergency was still going strong?

'Why, our lawyer even called yesterday to remind me,' Rish said.

'And *you* didn't remind *me*!' I screamed.

'Relax,' he said. 'Just breathe.'

'God,' I muttered and decided to call Ravi. There was no answer. I called Matthew and told him about the mix-up in dates and that I needed the day off for the divorce, after which I had to go to Mahabalipuram and then leave for the wedding. Matthew listened patiently and I couldn't tell how much he understood, but promised to take care of things at work. This is why it helped to be friends with client servicing people, no matter how much we hated them. They always had a better rapport with the boss and were darn good at coming up with sincere-sounding excuses.

Rish whistled as we drove to the family court.

'This is ridiculous,' I thought. 'We're just about to make the second most important decision of our lives next only to getting married and here he is, whistling. This isn't him and anything he does now, isn't him either.'

'How do you care?' my inner voice was back, 'You're getting what you want, aren't you?'

'I just want him to make an informed decision,' I shot back.

'Is that going to change your decision?'

'Just go away.'

We parked the car and made our way upstairs, looking for Mr Gopalakrishnan. The family court was in all manner of appearance, a blend of the market place and a government hospital – the crowds, the noise, the sweat, the arguments and a general feeling of despair that hung in the air; one look and I wanted to run. Rish on the other hand, kept walking on as if in one of London's scenic spots, whistling, with his head stuck in a big fat cloud of denial.

'Come, come!' Mr Gopalakrishnan greeted us eagerly as if he was throwing a party.

Rish shook his hand brightly and I smiled. We were then directed inside a room that felt every bit like the inside of an overcrowded PTC bus.

'With one billion people and counting, there isn't a single place in India you could go to without first standing in a queue,' I thought.

From all sides, people pressed against each other and like a lamb led to the slaughter, I followed Rish and found my own place in the crowd.

'You have to wait there till your names are called out,' Mr Gopalakrishnan informed us.

I held my stole to my nose, trying to drown out the odours in the room. With people pushing and shoving me from every side, I could tell almost every scent apart – jasmine flowers that made me sneeze incessantly, talcum powder, sweat, alcohol, paan, cigarette and even coconut chutney. I willed myself not to throw up and wished I didn't have such a keen sense of smell.

'S. Karunakaran and Vimala Karunakaran,' the lawyer called out from the table and a couple waved from the crowd.

'Anita Chander and Subash Chander,' he called out and a thin, scared-looking girl raised her hand.

I looked around hoping for some kind of explanation as to what was going on. I turned to Rish and I could tell he was humming, though I couldn't hear him over the noise.

'Only those who are present in the room right now will finish by afternoon,' a lady behind me explained to another.

'So this is like attendance in school,' I thought.

'Rishab Khanna and Deepika Sundar,' the lawyer finally called and we both waved and stepped out of the room. The corridor, which was also the waiting area, had long wooden benches that seated lawyers, anxious clients and distraught parents. On our right, Mr Gopalakrishnan paced back and forth on the phone, pretending to be busy. I looked around and noticed that Rish and I were the only couple that stood next to each other and did not look upset in the least.

'It should be over by lunch time,' our lawyer returned to reassure us and we continued waiting.

A woman in her fifties sat at the corner of the bench with a young girl who seemed like her daughter. The girl seemed all right, but the woman looked like she had lost everything and the world was coming to an end. I thought of our own parents and pictured them partying together at that very moment, on the way to the wedding. I wondered how they'd react when we made our announcement and within seconds, my head was caught up in a whirlpool of guilt, anxiety and painful doubt.

I turned to look at Rish, but he had moved away to speak to the lawyer by the balcony. I watched him from where I stood and let nostalgia do its thing – flood my mind with images of what was, what could have been, should have been and ought to have been. I fought the images with my best arguments, only to be presented by a whole new gamut of images – what still could be. Just then, Rish returned to my side and I looked at him, my eyes welled up and he looked back at me, humming *Mission Impossible*.

I opened my mouth to speak, but as it always happens in Tamil and Hindi flicks when the heroine is about to say something important, I was interrupted.

'Rishab Khanna and Deepika Sundar' someone called from another room and Mr Gopalakrishnan came bounding in our direction like a gleeful Labrador retriever.

'Your turn!' he announced pushing us into the room.

I knew that a divorce by mutual consent took place before a judge, in a simple, no-fuss way. But I had always pictured a full-fledged courtroom in my head. This on the other hand was something that resembled a corporation school classroom – a desk and chair for the judge, plain cement flooring and just enough room for six adults to stand. We stood before the judge as he clarified the information submitted to him and asked us in Tamil if we wished to be divorced.

'Yes,' we both answered without looking at each other.

He then asked us about property settlement and we nodded absent-mindedly that everything had been settled. He moved on to alimony and I said I did not require it.

'What? No alimony?' the judge looked shocked.

'No sir, I can support myself,' I confirmed.

'But this is wrong ma,' the judge was outraged at the thought of Indian women supporting themselves.

'You must insist on alimony,' he continued and looked at Rish with disgust.

Rish remained silent.

'Sir, I do not want alimony,' I said. 'Now can we please proceed?'

Reluctantly, the man asked us to sign one paper in addition to all the papers we had signed since morning and we followed through. He then pronounced us legally divorced, gestured for us to step outside the room and called out 'Next!'

Thirty-Four

Once out of the court, Rish and I barely exchanged words, or even eye contact. He followed the lawyer to his office, to give him the remainder of the payment and I rushed home to pack my bags and drive as quickly as I could to Mahabalipuram. I had to give that Guru a piece of my mind. I had to get him to make Rish return to normalcy. I wanted Rish to feel. I wanted him to do his share of worrying about telling the family. And when we finally did, I wanted him to be by my side, facing them, fielding questions and patiently explaining to them about how we got here. After all, we had both decided to convince the families. We both wanted their approval. But now it was just me and the sidekick of Guruji. Rish, the way I knew him, was no longer in the picture. I felt angry, alone and betrayed and I had only the Guru to blame.

It was late in the night when I reached the ashram, but a white hippie chick in a mustard kurta, capris and bandana, invited me in and enquired about the purpose of my visit. I told her I had to see the Guru and that it was urgent and she calmly explained that I had to wait until the next morning. I tried to argue, but realized she was another one of those brainwashed zombies that only knew how to smile. So I followed her into another room where she served me dinner – an all-vegetarian meal that had lemon rice, some vegetables that I couldn't identify and pickle. I thanked her and she sat by my side in silence, watching me eat.

'So, you are Rish's wife,' she finally said and I looked up, surprised.

'You know Rish?'

'Yes, I was the one who introduced him to Guruji,' she sounded pleased.

'I see,' I said and restrained myself from emptying the jar of water on her head.

When dinner was done, she showed me a small room that I could sleep in for the night and I thanked her. I stretched myself on the mat, but a series of bad dreams kept me up. The first one was of me working on the same shampoo brief at Bennet & Cole; everything around me had changed – the walls had different colours, the furniture looked swanky and futuristic and the computers appeared hi-tech; even the people were all different – no Matthew, Prathiba, Swetha, Mayura or even Ravi. I presented my ideas in the conference room and everyone laughed, holding their bellies. I ran outside and into the loo, to cry my eyes out and pray for the day to end, when I looked into the mirror. And that's what made me wake up, screaming – in the mirror, was a wrinkled, eighty-year-old version of me, still holding the brief of the shampoo ad.

I sat up and took in my surroundings. I checked the time – 3:23 a.m. 'This place is spooky,' I thought and went back to sleep. This time, the dream felt more like a short, two-minute clip of my life with Rish. It had the first long walk we took together when we got interested in each other, there was the rasgulla episode from IIM, our wedding day, our jokes, our Scrabble sessions, lovemaking and out of the blue, Rish smiling at me his eerie smile, wearing an orange garb and stroking his long beard. I sat up on my bed once again. The time was 5:56 a.m. I decided to wash up, get dressed and pound on the Guru's door by 6:00 a.m.

The Guru sat in his room, smiling as I entered.

'Rish's wife, aren't you?' he asked as I stepped forward.

I smiled. 'Ex wife,' I said, 'as of yesterday.'

'I've been waiting for you,' he said. 'Tell me, what brings you here?'

'I need you to fix Rish!' I gasped. 'Whatever you did to him, just fix him!'

Guruji smiled. 'Rish is all right, it's you who needs fixing.'

'Look Guruji,' I said, 'I don't have time for this. Rish has not been himself since he visited you and I just want you to please make him all right!'

'Close your eyes and try to keep your mind blank for a while,' he said in the same wispy tone that Rish spoke in.

I wanted to strangle him with his own beard but I obeyed.

'Does anything come to mind now?' he asked after what seemed like two minutes.

I thought for a while.

'My job,' I said, 'I hate it. But I don't have the money to support myself while I study to become a psychotherapist.'

'That is not your problem,' he said. 'What else?'

'What do you mean that is not my problem? I need a solution for that!'

'The solution will come when you fix the bigger problem,' he said calmly.

'Huh?' I opened my eyes.

Guruji stroked his beard again and smiled. 'Now tell me, how well do you sleep?'

I blinked.

'Close your eyes,' he said.

I closed my eyes and thought for a bit. 'I could sleep better I guess.'

'So, what is the one thing that gets in the way of your sleep every night?' he asked.

'You!' I said. 'You and Rish get in the way of my sleep, my peace, everything! You have brainwashed him and now he wants to join you! What will happen to his future? He's just not himself!' I ranted for a while.

'You're a touch too concerned for an ex-wife, don't you think?' Guruji asked, smiling.

'That's not the point, Guruji,' I said,'Rish has a problem.'

'When people come here, they come burdened. And when they finally release those burdens, they are afraid to go back into the world and face their current reality. So they seek to escape by hiding here. But that isn't the solution.'

It sounded like fla fla fla to me.

'I'm saying Rish will be fine,' he said. 'Now, is that all you came to see me about?'

'Yes,' I said but remained seated.

I looked around me tentatively. The place was unnervingly calm.

'Close your eyes,' Guruji said.

I obeyed.

'Have you heard of the Princess and the Frog?'

'What?' I said opening my eyes, 'How is that relevant?'

'Close your eyes,' he ordered again. I did.

'You fell in love with a prince. You divorced a frog.'

I rolled my eyes. 'With all due respect Guruji, what is your point?'

'So, is he a prince or a frog?'

'I don't know,' I answered.

'Well, you won't find the other answers you're looking for, till you answer this,' he said.

'This is ridiculous,' I thought but I was afraid he could read my mind.

'What about my future?' I asked. 'My desire to become a psychotherapist?'

'Everything is connected in the great, big circle of life,' the Guru said and I wondered if he memorized his lines from Disney. First, The Princess and the Frog and now, Lion King. He sounded like a sad, seventy-year-old wistful lover who got screwed over by Disney and was still waiting for his princess to whisk him into the sunset.

'Once you find the answer to the bigger question, this one will just resolve itself,' he said.

'And the bigger question is?' I opened my eyes.

'Prince or Frog,' the Guru smiled, his eyes twinkling.

Thirty-Five

When I entered our apartment, Rish was typing away furiously at his laptop. 'Hello, crazy ex-wife,' he said grinning at me over his laptop.

'Oh thank God he's back to normal,' I thought. 'The Guru was right.'

'What are you busy on the laptop for? It's time to pack and catch our flight, you know?' I said.

'The packing is done,' he said. 'Yours as well. We're good to go!'

'What?' I turned around, 'Did you just say we are ready ahead of time?'

'Mmmhmm,' he nodded, still working.

'And that you've actually packed your bag *and* mine?'

'I believe so,' he smiled, eyes still on the laptop.

'Prince,' I thought, smiling to myself.

'Wow, that is refreshing and out of character! I'm going to shower and get ready,' I said. 'What are you working on so intently though?'

'My first book,' he beamed.

'Ooh. What's it about?'

'The story of our marriage,' he smiled.

'Uhh . . .'

'Well, it does have a different ending,' he said.

'Definitely Prince,' I thought and headed for the shower.

The flight to Delhi was almost three hours and I looked forward to catching up on all my lost sleep. My prince however decided to beat me to it and kept me awake with his incessant snoring.

'Rish,' I shook him 'you're snoring too loudly.'

'Find another seat,' he snapped, still asleep.

'What did he think, this was a PTC bus?' I mumbled to myself.

'Frog,' I made a mental note.

About thirty minutes before landing, he was fresh, wide awake and grinning like a circus monkey and I was sleepy, cranky and intent upon saying or doing anything to wipe that grin off his face.

'So, how are we planning to break the news?' I asked him.

'I don't know,' he said, yawning, 'I don't have a plan.'

'Well, we need one if we are to convince them about our decision!'

'But we've already made the decision,' he said matter-of-factly.

'It was your idea to convince them!' I raised my voice and the aunty next to me stirred in her sleep, 'That's why it's taken us so long, in the first place!'

'It was your idea to get divorced!' he shot back and aunty was wide awake.

'What?' I couldn't believe him.

He shrugged, folded his arms and turned his face away like a complete grown-up.

'Look at me!' I ordered, 'I'm trying to have an adult conversation here.'

'Really? Where's the adult? Where? Where?' he placed his right hand against his forehead and did a mock search.

Aunty gawked at us, mouth open.

'Frog,' I decided. 'Through and through.'

When we reached Delhi, it was already about eleven in the night. We took an auto to Dimple aunty's place and argued all the way about whose idea the divorce was in the first place. I finally said that it did not matter, because it was a good idea and he agreed. We reached the house – an old colonial-looking bungalow that seemed freshly painted.

There was a large garden that looked like it hadn't been maintained in a while and an old green Fiat stood just outside.

'Looks like they could use a Honda City themselves,' I said, as we walked towards the house.

'Oh Raju uncle loves that Fiat,' Rish answered. 'He wouldn't give it up for a Rolls Royce Phantom.'

Multi-coloured fairy lights adorned every tree, shrub and leaf in the garden, making the entire house feel like one large shiny disco ball. It was past midnight, but we could tell the party was still going strong, given the loud music, laughter and cheering that emanated from the living room.

'Here they come!' the aunties, uncles and cousins from both sides howled and hooted as we entered the house, that it seemed like they had mistaken us for the bride and groom.

'If not for you two, there wouldn't be a wedding tomorrow,' Dimple aunty came running towards us while Raju uncle fed us sweets.

Rish and I exchanged a brief guilty look, when a few of Rish's younger cousins came forward to take our bags inside.

'Ah, Rish, Deepu, you're finally here!' my mother waved from the sofa in the corner of the room.

This was a strange setting for an Indian wedding. Both bride's side and groom's side stayed at the same house and partied together. There were no arguments, culture clashes or dowry negotiations.

'We really have set a trend,' I said to Rish. 'Look at them blending in so seamlessly, I can barely tell your people from mine.'

'I told you it makes a good story,' he said.

Just then, Reshu periamma pounced on Rish from behind and took him by his cheeks as usual.

'All thanks to you both,' she said, shaking him vigorously, 'I've got such a fair and lovely, milk-white, daughter-in-law.'

She waited as she always did, till Rish's cheeks changed colour and only then released him.

'Okay, *she*,' Rish said rubbing his cheeks in pain, 'does *not* blend in!'

I chuckled heartily and thought it served him right for all the snoring in the flight. Prince spotted Rish from the balcony and came to steal him away for a drink. I was tired at the thought of the next day's long and exhausting ceremony with all the dancing – that it only made me want to collapse on a bed as soon as I could. So I quickly made my way out of the living room before Twinky could find me and insist on a conversation about Robin, Rihanna or Bunty.

'Where are Kitty and Karthick?' I asked Dimple aunty as she took me upstairs to my room.

'Who knows?' she laughed, 'They must have gone for a walk. They are always trying to get away from the crowd, those two.'

I smiled. Dimple aunty went on her toes and kissed me on my forehead, when we were in the room.

'Such an adorable couple you two make,' she smiled. 'You've brought so much joy to both families. I just hope Kitty and Karthick are as happy.'

'Careful what you wish for' I thought to myself. Dimple aunty said good night and left the room.

I closed the door and looked at the baby pink, queen-size bed that beckoned me to dive in. I dropped my handbag, got out of my shoes and fell diagonally on it, drifting immediately into a deep, dreamless sleep.

Thirty-Six

When I woke up the next morning, the house seemed to be in panic-mode. I didn't quite know what was going on or even if there *was* something going on, but thanks to Guruji's influence, even from the quiet bedroom upstairs, I could tell there was a sense of unrest in the air. I sat up on my bed and surveyed the scene. The room looked just the way it did when I entered it the previous night. I examined the bed and I knew no one other than me had slept in it. Outside the room, I could hear the sound of footsteps pacing hastily back and forth.

'What now?' I wondered, 'Does a day go by without drama in this family?'

An old wooden clock on the wall indicated that it was well past breakfast time. In a couple of hours, we had to be at Kitty and Karthick's wedding ceremony and I was just getting out of bed. I felt oddly upset that no one had bothered to wake me up. I brushed, had a quick shower and got into my onion pink and cream lehenga that I had blown a huge portion of my monthly earnings on.

I checked out my reflection in the ornate, antique mirror that hung in the bathroom and decided I had enough shimmery sequins and crystals on me to pass for an authentic Punjabi bhabi. I then dabbed on some make-up and adjusted my hair one last time, to ensure I looked good enough for the hallowed halls of the Oberoi hotel, where the ceremony was to take place.

When I went down the stairs to the living room, the scene was nothing short of chaotic – all the aunties sat on the divan looking mournful and comforting Dimple aunty who seemed to be having an anxiety attack. In the garden, Reshu periamma stood ordering drivers, gardeners and electricians around. The men of the family walked in and out of the house, some nodded dramatically and others made frantic phone calls. Rish was nowhere to be seen. I reached for my phone and found a text from him, sent at 6:10 in the morning.

'Chaos,' it said.

I called him and there was no answer. I scanned the house for any of the cousins and nobody was around.

'Somebody please tell me what's going on!' I asked, unable to take the suspense anymore. Rimple aunty stretched out her hand and held out a note for me to read.

'Oh my God,' I thought, 'did somebody just leave a suicide note?'

Thanks to years of Indian cinema, notes always rang an ominous bell in my head.

Dear mom, dad, aunties, uncles and cousins,

We can't get married. We're sorry you're about to be embarrassed before your guests, but we can't do this now. We want to get to know each other better and be best friends like Rish (bhaiya) and Deepu (didi). We just don't feel ready yet. And if we got married now, we might not share the magic that they share and end up happy. We hope you'll forgive us.

Karthick & Kitty

'This is surely some kind of cosmic joke,' I thought to myself. I thought about the guests who were to be sent off, the money already spent and the bookings that couldn't be cancelled at the last minute. I was angry – with Karthick and Kitty for being so irresponsible; but more angry that Rish and I couldn't stop coming across as something we were clearly not.

I read the letter again and agreed they had made the right decision, though I didn't dare say it out loud. Cancelling a wedding at the last minute was still better than getting into a bad marriage.

'But define bad marriage,' my inner voice was back.

'Uhh, the one Rish and I were in?' I said.

'Wrong answer. Try again.'

I didn't have time for this game, so I tried to turn my attention to the crisis at hand.

'I'm sorry, but you two not being able to agree on a wall colour, does not qualify as a bad marriage in the adult world,' the inner voice continued.

'So that's what you think our problems were all about,' I asked. 'Wall colours?'

'Pretty much. Unless you count snoring , humming, kissing with bad morning breath, toilet seat, fa..'

'Shut up!' I cut her, 'What about him stealing my dream and becoming a writer?'

'Listen to yourself! You don't even *want* to be a writer anymore!'

'Fine. What about all the fights? We are always fighting!'

'And what do you fight about?'

I thought for a while and sheepishly admitted. 'Wall colours, snoring and morning breath.'

'Thank you,' she said. 'Now figure it out!'

'Figure what out?'

'Frog or Prince,' and she disappeared.

'Hey! Wait!' I screamed but she didn't come back.

Thirty-Seven

The garden soon filled up with people – relatives who lived close by and family friends who had decided to drop in home, before the wedding. I sat by myself in one of the plastic chairs outside, waiting to hear from Rish and wondering about what my inner voice had said.

'What a stupid boy he must be, to let go of a Honda City,' a fat lady in a red saree said to a group of women who sat around her.

'And Oberoi,' another one added. 'What a waste! I heard a single room costs about 20,000 rupees there!'

'I told Dimple that our Sonu will be a good match for Kitty,' a henna-haired woman joined the conversation.

'But she insisted on this Madrasi boy,' she added. 'Now look, what happened!'

All the women tch-tched and agreed that Madrasis were evil.

My phone rang. It was Rish.

'They're here,' he said, 'come to the India Gate Park. Just you.'

'Okay,' I answered and rushed outside to find an auto.

I barely knew my way around Delhi, but this one was easy enough to find. The auto took me straight to the park and I stepped down in my sequin-studded lehenga in the mid-afternoon sun, feeling like a complete moron.

The place was crowded, with families picnicking under the trees and lovers stealing kisses on the benches. Children ran about wildly in the play zone, their eyes gleaming with excitement. I held the two sides of my lehenga in my hands and walked towards the play area where Rish said he would meet me.

I rehearsed the speech I would give Kitty and Karthick in my head, one last time. I wanted to tell them that they will never feel ready. That there will always be someone who does it better. That they'll never quite know if this is really it. But they just might end up missing out on the best thing yet if they never tried.

'Hey,' Rish called out from behind me.

'Hey!' I turned around. There was no sign of Kitty or Karthick.

'You look more ravishing than you did on our wedding day,' he said.

I smiled. He was in sky blue jeans and a white tee. Obviously, he had heard of Kitty and Karthick's parting note well before he got dressed for the wedding.

'Where are they,' I asked and Kitty and Karthick stepped up from behind me.

I cleared my throat to make the speech, but they didn't give me a chance.

'We wanted to speak to both of you together,' Karthick said.

We moved to one of the benches and sat there.

'Okay,' I said and Rish nodded. 'We're listening.'

Kitty looked at me. 'You know how you can tell exactly how uncomfortable Rish bhaiya is, based on the tune he's humming?' Kitty asked me.

I smiled, 'Yes?'

'I want to be able to do that,' she said, 'with the guy I marry.'

'Bollocks. I don't hum when I'm uncomfortable,' Rish said and the three of us laughed.

'And you know how you deliberately delay every time you're getting ready to leave somewhere,' Karthick said to Rish, 'because you think she's so cute when she gets worked up?'

'You deliberately delay?' I asked.

'Yeah, but I don't think you're cute,' he winked.

'And the way you two are always a team, always trying to get away from the crowd to be together,' Kitty said. 'Everyone in the family wants a marriage like yours!'

'That part is because the family gives us no choice,' I thought to myself.

'What we're trying to say is,' Karthick said, 'Kitty and I don't know each other at all. And when we look at you . . .' he trailed off.

'You guys are best friends,' Kitty said, 'and we just don't want to settle for anything less than that.'

'Well, best friends can sometimes make you want to kill them,' Rish warned.

'True,' I nodded.

'Well then you just go for a smoke and get back when you don't feel like killing them,' Karthick said matter-of-factly.

'True,' Rish agreed.

'So, what are we going to do now?' I asked everyone.

'I want to move to Chennai and get to know Karthick better,' Kitty said.

'I meant, right now, about the wedding,' I said.

Everyone was silent.

'You guys never had a Punjabi wedding party did you?' Karthick had a brainwave.

Kitty's face lit up as she thought of all the possibilities, 'That is true!'

Rish and I looked at each other.

'We could do "Two States – The Punjabi Chapter" right here at the Oberoi!' Kitty continued.

I swallowed. I needed to be alone with Rish. I needed to talk to him.

'You guys go on and we'll be right behind,' Rish said to Karthick and Kitty, as if reading my mind.

The minute Karthick and Kitty were out of sight, I knelt down.

'Rishab Khanna,' I said. He raised his eyebrows at me.

'What are you doing?' he tried to lift me up.

'Shhh,' I said. 'Just hear me out.'

He stood before me, trying not to look embarrassed, even as passers-by gawked at us in amusement.

'Rishab Khanna,' I started over, 'you are my prince *and* my frog.'

'Huh?' he said.

'Shhh. Just go with me!' I ordered and he kept silent.

'You are messy, annoying, forgetful and even irresponsible,' I started.

He nodded and listened.

'You snore too loudly, think fart jokes are funny, you buy towels with ogres on them thinking they are cute, you kiss before brushing your teeth and you watch Star Trek,' I continued.

'I'm guessing this is going to get better, because you're on your knees,' he said.

'But you also kiss me and stroke my hair after I go to sleep, every time we have a fight and I *know*, because I'm never asleep when you do it,' I said.

He smiled.

'And though IIT gave you a Gandhi complex and you think you're going to change the future of the nation, I love how you need my opinion on every little thing you do.'

'I do not have a Gandhi complex,' he protested.

A group of college boys whistled as they passed us, but I continued.

'And you always buy the raspberry flavour Absolut though you like the orange flavour, because you know I love raspberry.' My voice broke and two drops of tears trickled down my cheeks.

Rish chuckled and lifted me up.

'I like raspberry,' he said and kissed me.

'Wait!' I said, 'I'm not done yet.'

'Sorry, go on.'

'And I know we have a very high-schoolish relationship, but you are my calmer and I like the fact that I feel so much younger when I'm with you.'

'Good justification for all the spit-balls you blow at me when I'm trying to work,' he said.

'So, Rishab Khanna,' I said, 'will you marry me again, so we can grow younger together?'

He laughed. 'Oh well. I hate making a woman beg.'

Thirty-Eight

When we got back home with Kitty and Karthick, everyone was hopping mad. The uncles refused to look at them, the aunty-gathering in the garden tch-tched and the women in the family pulled one of their hand-on-chest, 'How could you bring such shame upon us' drama. Karthick shuffled his feet and Kitty began to weep. Rish and I looked at each other and we knew we had to whip up another one of our youngsters-teaching-the-elders speeches to get them to see the light.

'What happened was a mistake,' Rish began, 'one that has cost a lot of money and Kitty and Karthick are aware of that *and* they are sorry.'

'Money?' Reshu periamma said, 'What about all the shame, the embarrassment in front of friends and relatives?'

'What is there to be ashamed of?' Rish argued, 'It's not like they've dumped an illegitimate baby at your doorstep!'

'The sangeet is already over,' I stepped in. 'They just need time to get to know each other, so they can be sure of what they're doing and make their married life happy!'

'There is nothing to get to know,' Raju uncle said. 'What they know is enough!'

'Only if they get married, they'll know what happiness is,' Rimple aunty said but Chandu uncle didn't look like he agreed.

'Look,' Rish said calmly, 'I understand you're angry and you have a right to be, but if they get married now, they could end up unhappy and divorced.'

A collective tch-tch swept across the family at the mention of the 'D' word.

'So *you* decide if you're going to be angry with them forever,' I said for added effect.

The elders then discussed among themselves for five minutes and Raju uncle came forward to hug Kitty. Then Reshu periamma hugged Karthick and everyone hugged everyone and there was a lot of kissing, crying, hugging and peace-making.

'So, what about all the arrangements we've made?' Raju uncle asked looking like a disappointed puppy.

'Well, we could still celebrate,' I said.

'Celebrate what?' Dimple aunty asked and I could sense the air growing thick again. We needed a strategy and right away.

'Actually, Rish and I have an announcement to make,' I said and Rish looked nervous.

Everyone fell silent and listened intently.

'We are both switching careers,' I said, hoping they would consider that a cause for celebration.

There was silence. Everyone looked anxious and confused.

'I want to become a novelist,' Rish stepped in.

'And I want to study and start afresh as a psychotherapist,' I added.

All the cousins clapped and cheered, but the elders ignored me and pounced on Rish.

'You're throwing away your successful career to write stories?' Chandu uncle asked.

'You mean, all your IIT education is of no use now?' Reshu periamma asked.

'All our efforts have gone to waste!' his mother sniffed.

I looked at Rish and knew it was damage control time. Rish was a patient guy but once he lost it, he really lost it . . . Any more drama and I could tell he would have just broken a flower pot over someone's head.

'I'm pregnant!' I blurted out before the common-sense part of my brain could approve it.

Twinky let out her signature shriek and immediately, the thickness in the air dissolved; and the aunties along with my mother praised the goddesses of fertility and rejoiced that the barrenness curse was finally lifted.

Rish looked confused and horrified.

'Now this calls for a celebration at the Oberoi hotel!' Reshu periamma said and everyone agreed.

'Also, they never had a Punjabi reception,' Kitty said and the entire family ran to get dressed and hit the venue.

'What the hell were you doing?' Rish asked me halfway through the dancing when we were both comfortably drunk.

A re-mix version of a 70s Bollywood number blared from the speakers.

'I don't know,' I gasped, my hands in the air, 'but we better make a baby tonight, Rishab Khanna.'

'Dropping out of MBA, fake suicide attempt, secret divorce and now an illegitimate child,' he said. 'The things you make me do.'

'True love does come at a heavy price,' I said.

'True. It roughly costs about forty thousand rupees,' he said and we both laughed thinking of Mr Gopalakrishnan.

'So, when are we getting married, hot-shot novelist?' I asked.

'As soon as we head back home, *psycho* therapist,' he winked.

Thirty-Nine

I took my time before getting back to work, when we reached Chennai. Rish and I had a lot of conversation to catch up on and loose ends to tie. And most importantly, rules had to be laid down if we were to give another shot at a life together and especially, if that life included a baby.

'Farting aloud is not funny,' I said, stretching myself on the couch, my feet on his lap.

'Okay,' he said, playing with my toes, 'and brushing before making love is a mood killer.'

'Fine,' I agreed.

'You should get nose strips for your snoring,' I suggested.

'Or you could get ear plugs.'

'Or you could just sleep on the couch.'

'Fine, I'll get nose strips.'

'You don't have to come shopping with me, if I don't have to watch *Star Trek* with you.'

'Deal!' He sounded relieved.

Then we went on to confession time – all those little white lies we had said to make life easier, the nice things about each other that we never shared because we were too busy being resentful, the many minor irritations that we kept to ourselves and the many chronic issues we swept under the rug on a daily basis.

'I still think you look like George Clooney's younger bro,' I said, beginning the confession on a positive note.

'I still have the hots for Shilpa Shetty,' he reciprocated.

'You know,' I hesitated, 'I'm not one of those women who likes pillow talk. I'd rather fall asleep after making love.'

He was silent.

'I'm sorry,' I said.

'You know, this is so tragic, it's oddly funny,' he said after a few seconds.

I looked at him quizzically.

'I've been trying so hard to keep awake, cuddle and make conversation, because I thought that's what women wanted!'

'You mean you don't like pillow talk either?' I asked, completely baffled.

'No! Which guy with two testicles in good working condition wants to talk about his *feelings* after sex?'

'Wow,' I chuckled, 'this is turning into an O'Henry story.'

'Who the hell is O'Henry?'

I laughed out loud. 'And you're planning on becoming a novelist! Maybe you should call your first book that – "Who the hell is O'Henry?" '

'Oh, I have little interest in impressing the starchy-cotton-saree-clad fifty-somethings, who like to sip green tea and discuss literature,' he said, putting on his signature condescending air. 'I am going to write in a way that does not intimidate people. I am going to make India read!' he continued.

'Gandhi complex,' I pointed out.

'Oh whatever. You're just lucky you won't be my evil ex-wife when I'm India's highest-selling author.'

'Okay and this is the point where the cockiness stops being charming and gets downright annoying,' I said.

'So you don't believe I can do this?'

'Of course I do,' I said. 'It'll be great though, if you can let *me* do the believing while *you* focus on the writing.'

He smiled.

'Okay, so here's the plan. I work and write and you quit and study,' he said.

'What? Are you sure?' I hadn't expected this to be so easy.

He nodded, smiling.

'Oh my God! Thank you!' I threw my arms around him, 'The Guru was right!'

'What?' he asked, 'What did the Guru say?'

'Oh it's nothing. He said my career problem will resolve itself once I figured out if you were my frog or prince.'

'What?' he asked, 'The Guru told you *that*?'

'Mmhm.'

'The Guru knows his fairy tales?' he asked again.

'Looks like it!' I smiled.

'Do me a favour darling? Please don't turn the one sane guy on earth, into a nut job? Stay away from him, I pray you.'

And we spent the next eighteen hours on the couch – chatting, confessing, laying down rules, taking them back, discovering each other and falling in love. This time, for keeps. We then headed to the court to submit our photos and other certificates for a registered marriage and waited with bated breath, like eloped lovers for our day to come.

When I got back to work, it was to put in my papers. I was thrilled to bits about my life working itself out in a day and I couldn't wait to tell my disappointed colleagues that Rish and I were getting married again.

I was feeling guilty about quitting though, as everyone had been extremely understanding of my situation and I thought I'd offer to stay for as long as it took them to replace me. But when I entered my workplace with my big news, the scene was radically different – it was only 10:30 in the morning and everyone was in the office; there were no Facebook pages open and nobody was standing by the coffee machine, chatting.

There were no paper rockets flying around or music blaring from the speakers. I tip-toed my way to Swetha and Prathiba and they both informed me that the shampoo launch was a complete disaster – the copywriter hadn't proofread the ads before they went to print, the prints came out with mistakes in the headline, the colours were smudged on the banners, the inflatable didn't work and the emcee fell sick.

Needless to say, the client who was a big name in the FMCG arena, was hopping-mad at the agency and decided to fire us. The south head, national head and every head of every department had come down to speak to the client and straighten the mess, but nothing could be done.

So, Ravi was in his room that very moment with Meera Swaminathan, VP South, calling people in to either fire them or let them go with a serious warning. Apparently, there wasn't a single soul in the agency who didn't have a part to play in The Great 26/10 Shampoo Tragedy.

I nodded and opened my mail.

'So, you and Rish,' Swetha asked, 'you guys are divorced yet?'

'Mmhmm,' I nodded.

'Okay,' they both said and focussed on their respective computers.

'But, we're getting married again in a month and I'm going to need you guys as witnesses!' I whispered, winking.

'What?' Prathiba asked, 'Your families still don't know anything?'

'No,' I shook my head.

They giggled. 'This is so exciting. I feel like I'm back in high-school!' Swetha said.

'Yeah, she makes up for my uneventful, single life,' Prathiba added.

Just then, the door opened ominously and Ravi stepped out of the room. He caught us giggling and asked to see me inside. I shrugged and followed him. I loved the sense of liberation that came with knowing I didn't need the job anymore.

'Meera,' he began, 'this is Deepika. Senior Copywriter. You might have met.'

'Yes, I think we've met,' she said politely.

'So, let's cut to the chase,' she said.

'Yes!' I said a little more cheerfully than I should have.

'Which part of the launch did you handle?'

'Actually,' I started.

'Deepika was away because of a personal crisis,' Ravi explained.

'Yes, I was getting divorced,' I said.

'Oh I'm so sorry,' Meera said, her hand on her chest and looking like she could hug me.

She was a tall, dark woman about forty-five years old, known in advertising circles for her authoritative demeanour and general coldness with colleagues and subordinates. At this moment though, Meera was just another Indian aunty who got palpitations at the mention of the 'D' word.

'Oh it's all good,' I said. 'We're getting married again!'

This was when she was supposed to go 'awwww' but suddenly she didn't seem to think it was cute. She thought I was taking her for a ride and what's more, she thought Ravi was an idiot for having bought my stories all this while. She turned her signature now-get-out-of-my-sight face to Ravi and gave him what I presumed was an eye signal.

'Uhhh,' Ravi cleared his throat, 'that's good for you Deepika, but I'm afraid we have to let you go.'

I smiled.

'I'm sorr . . . .'

'Thank you!' I jumped from my seat. I hugged both of them and came bounding out of the room delightfully, like I just swapped designations with Meera.

Everyone looked at me with fear, suspicion and loathing as if I had just been promoted as evil lord over them all.

'No more shampoos and jojoba for me, guys!' I squealed, 'I just got fired!'

And suddenly, I was the girl who got divorced, fired and turned mental and everyone wanted to be my friend. Very touching it was, but I had a degree to work for and a pining, soon-to-be second husband to get back to. So I hugged Matthew, Swetha, Prathiba and Mayura, blew kisses to everyone else and ran as fast as I could from Bennet & Cole and the ad world itself – full of its unreasonable clients, laughable briefs and shampoo emergencies.

I was on my way to delving headlong into the human psyche and becoming the psycho I knew I was and the therapist I hoped I could be.

Forty

'And that is the story of my divorce,' I said.

Sid removed his glasses and wiped a tear.

'Beautiful!' he said, 'Just beautiful,' and shook his head dramatically.

'Now, can you give me that report saying I'm ready for a divorce?'

'What? Did my story mean nothing to you?'

'Of course it did. It reassured me that my wife and I are nothing like you and Rish,' he said. 'And that's the point of therapy right? Being at peace with yourself?'

'Hmmm,' I thought, 'I *am* really good at this.'

'Except,' he added, 'I was sure even before I came here, but now that I've coughed up two thousand rupees, I'm 100 per cent sure.'

My urge to slap him was back on.

It had been almost four hours and Sid was now comfortably stretched on the divan against my fuschia wall and showed no sign of budging.

'We still have ten minutes,' he informed me.

'Do *you* want to talk this time?' I asked him bored.

'You still haven't finished your story,' he said. 'Did you have the baby?'

I sighed. 'Looks like I should give up this career as well for telling stories to mentally deranged individuals like yourself,' I said.

He laughed.

'Come on,' he cajoled. 'Finish the story.'

'Fine,' I said and cleared my throat. He put on his attentive-terrier face.

'We had a boy the following year and a girl, two years later,' I said.

'Wow. Did you call them Monty and Python?' he grinned.

'Shut up,' I said.

'Oh wait. Pimple and Nipple?'

'Siddharth Mehta,' I said, 'are you making fun of your own clan?'

'I believe so,' he said, 'thanks to you.'

'So back to my story – Aryan is now four and has his father's Gandhi complex and Rhea is two and mostly just awesome. Like me.'

'Wah, wah,' Sid nodded. We had one more minute.

'Okay, last question,' he begged.

'Shoot,' I said.

'So, Rish went to IIT and you went to Stella Maris. Where do you want your kids to go – IIT? One of the top B schools? Or our very own Loyola and Stella Maris College?

'They will go to a school called life,' I said.

Epilogue

'Rinky! Rinky! Don't go there, beta!' a very flustered-looking Twinky, adjusted her sequin and crystal studded saree and ran after her youngest child Rihanna who had just begun walking.

We were at the Oberoi, Delhi, again and this time, the wedding was actually happening.

'Come, come! Deepu! Rish!' Reshu periamma dazzled in an orange and gold, Kanjeevaram Pattu Saree.

'Where are those edible little babies of yours?' she had now made a ritual of pinching Aryan and Rhea's cheeks instead of Rish's and Rish didn't know whether to be relieved or even more disturbed.

'Such fair children,' she continued, 'come here, Aryan, come, come!'

Aryan and Rhea hid under the rasgulla table on the sprawling lawn and Aryan, signalled to me to keep quiet.

'History repeats itself,' I thought and smiled to myself.

The Old Wives Club was busy attacking the chaat table and Rish's father sat drinking at the bar with mine. Both men looked engrossed in conversation and I was glad they had finally found each other. Arvind had grown a whole foot taller and walked around in a kurta, greeting everyone and making the high-school girls giggle and point at him.

'So much has changed,' I said to Rish who now stood next to me, sipping his drink.

'Rishab Khanna?' a whole group of young things flocked around Rish.

'I've read all your books!' a college girl oozed admiration.

'I never liked reading till I read your books,' another twenty-something girl said.

'Can we have your autograph?' they asked.

Rish modestly obliged and I stood by him and smiled, every bit like the surprised woman behind this successful man who had in fact, made India read.

'So much has changed,' Rish agreed when the group had left.

The wedding went on well into the night and Twinky, Prince, Rish and I, spent most of it looking for Aryan, Rhea, Bunty, Lotu and Rinky under tables, inside fountains and behind huge stone carvings.

'I cannot believe I signed up for this,' I said, when we finally got to sit down and rest our heels.

'Are you kidding? I can't get enough! We're having one more!' Twinky announced perkily pointing to her tummy.

'No!' I said in disbelief. I had thought it was just the extra weight from her previous pregnancies.

'You're a brave woman, Twinky!'

'Say hello to Robin!' she shrieked.

'Uhh, so it's final?' I asked, 'You're actually naming your daughter Robin?'

'We'll be calling her Binky, of course,' she said matter-of-factly and got up to look for Prince.

My eyes darted across the hall, from one happy scene to the next – I looked at Karthick and Kitty posing for photographs – every bit in love, Twinky waddling with her fifth-month belly, Arvind turning heads, my father and pop-in-law laughing over a drink, The Old Wives Club animatedly discussing their next get-together and groups of young people pointing at Rish who was wrestling with Aryan while Rhea hung on his neck.

'All is well,' I thought to myself.

'Deeps!' Rish called from the food counter and I suddenly remembered I hadn't eaten.

'Here. I saved some for you from your ravenous brats,' Rish handed me the last bite of rasgulla left on his plate.

'Awww,' I said, 'you saved me the last bite of rasgulla!'

'And some things never change,' he winked.

And we all lived cornily ever after.

* * *